The two gunmen joined in, tackling Ki in a pile. Already weakened, Ki could not hold them off. A well-aimed gun butt struck the back of his head, and again, harder, and Ki dropped flat. They smashed his ribs and battered his face, breaking his bones with their heavy boots.

"Don't kill him!" Jessie screamed, helpless in the grip of the two thugs. "Let him go!"

At a nod from their leader, one of the killers cocked his revolver and stooped, placing the muzzle at Ki's temple. "Make up your mind, my sweet," said the ringleader. "Either you marry me willingly, or Ki dies—here and now . . ."

DON'T MISS THESE
ALL-ACTION WESTERN SERIES
FROM THE BERKLEY PUBLISHING GROUP

THE GUNSMITH by J. R. Roberts
Clint Adams was a legend among lawmen, outlaws, and ladies. They called him . . . the Gunsmith.

LONGARM by Tabor Evans
The popular long-running series about U.S. Deputy Marshal Long—his life, his loves, his fight for justice.

LONE STAR by Wesley Ellis
The blazing adventures of Jessica Starbuck and the martial arts master, Ki. Over eight million copies in print.

SLOCUM by Jake Logan
Today's longest-running action Western. John Slocum rides a deadly trail of hot blood and cold steel.

→◆→ WESLEY ELLIS ◆←

LONE STAR

AND THE DEATH MINE

JOVE BOOKS, NEW YORK

LONE STAR AND THE DEATH MINE

A Jove Book / published by arrangement with
the author

PRINTING HISTORY
Jove edition / December 1993

ISBN: 0-515-11256-9

A JOVE BOOK®.
Jove Books are published by The Berkley Publishing Group,
200 Madison Avenue, New York, New York 10016.
JOVE and the "J" design are trademarks
belonging to Jove Publications, Inc.

PRINTED IN THE UNITED STATES OF AMERICA

10 9 8 7 6 5 4 3 2 1

★

Chapter 1

That evening there was no twilight. The day had started in hot golden sunlight, but by noon, a single, high-altitude cloud of sluggish gray, like a vaporous sheet of dirty muslin, had crept across the heavens from the southwest. During the afternoon, as the stage rolled through the hill country east of San Antonio, Jessica Starbuck and her companion Ki would look out of the coach windows and see the cloud growing bloated and ugly. Accompanying it was a gusty rush of wind, both portents of a late summer cloudburst. What was coming was not an autumnal howler, but a short, swift deluge to cleanse the charged atmosphere.

Around evening, the road leveled off, winding through a canyon that was flanked by round-topped slopes dotted with oak, and then curved into the small town of Parumph. The town was hardly more than a glorified relay station for the stage line, the road becoming a main street lined by cabin-sized houses and small shops with slack-hipped stoops and tilted railings. Smack-dab in the middle of Parumph was the stage depot, the weathered clapboards of its livery stable and ticket office bulking like a huge misshapen box. Directly across the street stood the town's only hotel, grandly misnamed the DeLuxe—a two-storied falsefront with a sagging wood gallery running along the front.

By the time Jessie and Ki alighted from the stage, the sky was completely overcast, blanketed by muggy gray curds blistered with olive and purple, blotting out the sunset. Here in Parumph they had to switch to another stagecoach that would take them to Fort Younger, a day's ride away. And looking at the sky and feeling her aching bones, Jessie was relieved that the stage would be leaving tomorrow morning, and that they would be staying the night here, as poor as the hotel appeared.

Nonetheless, a good part of her was impatient to reach Fort Younger. It was there, in the fort's brig, that Lieutenant Gregory Nehalem was being held for murder. Greg Nehalem was the son of Eustace Nehalem, who had been a close friend and business associate of Jessie's late father, Alex Starbuck. A few years older than Jessie—closer in age to Ki—Greg Nehalem had as a child often played with Jessie, but as they had grown older, they had drifted apart, and Jessie had not seen Greg in quite a few years. From time to time she'd heard word about him—that his father had died, that he'd joined the Army, things like that—and then just a couple of weeks ago, she had read in a San Antonio newspaper that Greg had been arrested for shooting a Chinese merchant in the back.

2

Appalled, Jessie had written Major Veblen, the C.O. at Fort Younger, for confirmation. Replying, the major supplied Jessie with a condensed version of the report and evidence he was forwarding to Washington, along with the news that Lieutenant Nehalem would face court-martial on August 26. That was tomorrow. Business had prevented Jessie from traveling any sooner, but she was determined to be on hand for the court-martial, and to do everything in her power to help her childhood chum whatever the outcome. And she simply couldn't believe that Greg was guilty of shooting a man in the back. Something was definitely wrong.

Now, as she and Ki walked across to the hotel, the first stray handful of rain fell in big drops, like skinned grapes in the thick dust—a portent, Jessie thought, of worse to come. Upon entering the lobby, they were greeted effusively by the desk clerk, a chinless man with watery eyes, yellow teeth, and a few wisps of hair combed flat across his skull.

"Jessica Starbuck and Ki," Jessie declared, beginning to sign the register. "Adjoining rooms, please."

"Yes'm, yes'm, adjoining rooms." Grinning, the clerk grabbed a couple of keys from the rack behind him. "Twelve for you, Miz Starbuck, an' fourteen for your gentleman friend. Ground floor, at the end of the passage."

It was certainly a deferential reception, which Jessie was used to, except the clerk was laying on the smarm and bullshit overly thick, she thought. Toting their traveling bags—Jessie had a small

3

bellows case, and Ki carried a gladstone—they headed for the hallway. Some of those who happened to be in the lobby just then gave the pair the twice-over, often as not directed mostly at Jessie— the men admiring and the women envious of her striking beauty. Still in her twenties, she moved with lithe, regal grace, her taut, full breasts swelling her stylish two-piece outfit of light pearl-gray wool. Her leghorn hat hid the coils of her coppery-blond tresses, but the hat's wide brim did little to conceal her cameo face, with its pert nose, dimpled chin, and audacious green eyes.

Equally intriguing was Ki. A lean-featured man with bronze skin, blue-black hair, and almond eyes, he exuded a magnetic quality that suggested he was capable of strong loyalty when it was earned, and unstoppable ferocity when he was provoked. Born to the Japanese wife of an American sailor, then orphaned as a boy in Japan, he'd been trained in martial arts and the other skills of a samurai. Though he packed no firearm, the waistcoat and pockets of his brown traveling suit carried short daggers and other small throwing weapons, including the razor-sharp, star-shaped steel disks known as *shuriken*.

When Ki had first immigrated to America, he'd placed his talents in the service of Alex Starbuck. Consequently, he and Jessie had virtually grown up together, and after her father's murder, it seemed only fitting for him and Jessie to continue together. They were as affectionate and trusting as any blood-related brother and sister could be. They made a formidable team.

4

Walking along the corridor, they came to a door with the number 12 put on it with paint that looked like tar. Jessie was just about to insert her key in the door lock when abruptly she became conscious of an acrid, pungent smell that a chance draft, perhaps, had wafted to her nostrils.

"What's that smell? Or is it my imagination?"

Beside her, Ki took a whiff. He, too, detected the unpleasant odor; it reminded him of scorched cow turds. "Cigar smoke," he judged. "The cheapest six-for-a-quarter cigar at that." He stepped down the hall, went the other way a few paces, then returned to the door. "That's odd. The smell isn't anywhere except right here, as though it's seeping out from under the door."

"Well?"

"Well, don't go in. Not just yet."

In folks who ride much with deadly danger as a constant stirrup companion, there develops a subtle sense that often warns of peril when none is apparently present. Both Jessie and Ki had that sense strongly developed. And now the voiceless monitors in their brains were clamoring for attention. To plant a ruthless killer inside the room to shoot them as they entered would be a simple and easy way to eliminate them—although what motive, what reason, might be behind such an attempt utterly mystified them.

Careful not to make undue noise, Jessie reached into her chatelaine purse for her twin-shot derringer. Then, changing her mind, she left her derringer be, opened her bellows bag, and took out the custom Colt pistol she had

5

packed along, desiring its greater firepower. She leveled it ready as Ki unlocked the door and gently grasped the knob. The door opened outward. A swift turn of the knob, a hard jerk, and he could fling it open. The unexpectedness of the happening would tend to throw off balance anybody hiding in the room and waiting for him to enter.

With one swift, supple movement, Ki put the thought into action. The door slammed open, banging against the wall.

There was a thundering crash, a gush of flame. Buckshot screeched through the opening. The door across the hall splintered with a prodigious smashing and crunching of wood paneling. Smoke boiled from the room.

Jessie slammed back along the wall a half dozen steps, pistol out, her thumb hooked over the cocked hammer. Every nerve strung to the tightness of stretched wire, Ki waited with her, his eyes trained on the door. Nothing happened. In her room was utter silence. They could hear the muffled shouts of the aroused people back in the lobby. They waited for the thud of feet inside the room that would indicate that the gun wielder was seeking to escape by way of the window, but no sound came to them.

Ki's glance flickered past the open door and abruptly centered on a length of twine dangling from the inside doorknob. Instantly he understood. "Look, Jessie," he said, approaching the open door, and he stepped boldly into the room, Jessie a step behind him. They stopped abruptly, staring into

6

the twin muzzles of a sawed-off shotgun.

"String tied to the doorknob," Jessie noted. "If I'd opened the door to step into the room, I'd have gotten both barrels dead center. That's just what would've happened, if whoever set up this trap hadn't smoked a stinky cigar as he was working. I can't imagine why it was set up at all, though."

"We better find out," Ki said grimly, "before another try is made. Our luck can't hold out forever."

The open window showed how the would-be killer had gained entrance to the room. He had doubtlessly left the same way, after rigging the shotgun trap.

Boots pounded in the hallway. Men boiled into the room, some with guns out and ready. They took in the situation at a glance and exclaimed explosively as they examined the devilish contraption lashed to the bedpost. "We heard it let go," one of the men declared. "Didn't know what had busted loose!" Another cried, "Of all the pizenous, fangin' sons of Tophet! Ma'am, yuh shore had a close call!" A third queried, "How come it didn't git yuh? Them muzzles are trained to down anybody who opened the door."

Jessie explained just what happened.

"You got a keen nose," a man said, sniffing. "Reckon the hellion must've been keepin' tabs on y'all, and figured it'd be easy to slip in here to rope up this contraption."

"But how'd he know I'd be given this room?" Jessie asked.

Ki glanced sharply at her. "The clerk!"

7

As a group, they rushed back to the lobby, Jessie and Ki in the lead. The desk clerk was nowhere to be seen. Jessie turned to the men. "Anyone know who the clerk is? What's his name? Where does he live?"

There was a chorus of no's and shaking of heads. One chap spoke up: "He ain't the reg'lar clerk, ol' Prib. He told me Prib had gotten sick of a sudden, and he was just fillin' in. I dunno for sure, but seems to me Prib lives in the rear, in a back room there." The man gestured toward the door in the wall behind the desk.

"Well, let's check," Jessie said, heading for the door.

The back room proved to be living quarters, all right. It was a dark, cramped, squalid mess that appeared not to have been cleaned since the Civil War. Against the side wall was an iron bedstead, and lying on its thin mattress was the clothed body of an elderly man. A hatchet was wedged in his skull.

"That's Prib," the chap said, gagging.

Jessie, averting her eyes, said, "It's obvious that the clerk was murdered so that someone could take his place and put me in room twelve. That still doesn't answer why, of course. Maybe we'll never know. Right now, is there a sheriff or lawman of some sort in town?"

"Gottlieb," someone declared. "He's the agent over at the stage depot, and's appointed as acting deputy marshal hereabouts. I'll fetch him."

As the man hastened out of the hotel, Jessie stood with Ki and stared out of the lobby's front windows. For a fleeting moment she considered checking for footprints under her room's window, but the storm had broken and would have washed out any sign by now. It was falling with a sudden steady rain, no thunder or lightning or threshing of wind, just a heavy sodden downpour.

It fit the occasion.

★

Chapter 2

Gottlieb proved as useful as tits on a boar. He
chalked up Prib's murder to some old, unknown
score that had finally been settled, and took the
attitude toward the shotgun trap that "furriners
passin' through" like Jessie deserved whatever
they got. With that, he arranged a burial party
for Prib and went back to his drinking at a local
tavern.

The rest of the night passed uneventfully.

Next morning, Jessie and Ki boarded the stage
that would take them to Fort Younger. They had
changed to more workaday clothes, Jessie wearing
a plain silk blouse and form-hugging jeans and
jacket. Her derringer was now concealed behind
the wide square buckle of her belt, and her pistol was now holstered at her thigh. Ki was now
clad in denims, a collarless cotton-twill shirt, and
moccasin-style slippers. The weapons from his suit
he'd secreted in the many pockets of a worn leather vest.

About noon, the coach lost a front hub nut and
was laid up close to four hours. As a result, they
arrived at the fort very late in the day—too late,

Jessie feared, to attend the court-martial of Lieutenant Gregory Nehalem.

Established in June, 1836, Fort Younger was a link in the frontier defense system and helped to guard the San Antonio–Houston Trail. Like many such posts, it consisted of troop billets, warehouse, stable and farrier's shed, and a centrally located commandant's headquarters, all enclosed by a heavy stockade with blockhouses at opposite corners. A warm wind was blowing up as Jessie and Ki walked from the stage depot to the headquarters building, where an orderly stood outside the door. Jessie announced that she wanted to pay her respects to Major Veblen, in command.

In a moment the orderly returned wearing a broad smile. Jessie and Ki followed him into the building and found Major Veblen behind a long table, studying a stack of carefully penned reports. A trim man, the major was wearing a field "undress" uniform with the leaves of his rank. His hair was gray and still very thick, his face sun-blackened, spade-bearded, and humorless as he arose from his desk and extended his hand.

"A pleasure meeting you, Miss Starbuck, and you, Ki," he said after introductions. "I'm just sorry it has to be on so serious an occasion. Oh, and meet Mr. Ruther, Quaid Ruther, whose freight outfit supplies our sutlers hereabouts."

For the first time Jessie noticed the man who stood against a far wall. Garbed in the traditional plaid workshirt, twill pants, and flat-heeled boots of a teamster, Quaid Ruther was ruddy-haired and mustached, and had the height and brawn of an

Irish bruiser combined with the leaner, darker features of a Latin—a not uncommon byproduct of railroad laboring in the Southwest. Some time past, his nose had been broken and had healed crookedly, giving the bridge an S curve and his bushy brows a perpetual scowl, shadowing his deep-socketed, obsidian-bright eyes.

Ruther acknowledged them with a grunted nod, then turned to Veblen. "Well, guess I best be rollin' on my way, Major. Waitin' around here to testify at Nehalem's trail has put a real crimp in my schedule." With another nod to Jessie and Ki, he put on a black, flat-topped hat. He was halfway to the door when Jessie asked the major a question:

"Then we got here too late for the court-martial?"

"Afraid so, Miss Starbuck."

"What was the verdict?"

"Life. It was Nehalem's record that spared him from hanging. Life at the Brownsville stockade—er, at Fort Brown."

Pausing, Quaid Ruther complained in a growl, "But that was cold, deliberate murder."

"So the facts might indicate," Veblen said with a scowl.

"You mean to say there's some doubt of his guilt?" Jessie asked.

"I've known First Lieutenant Nehalem for a long time," Veblen said. "He's a good officer, and—"

"And a convicted killer," Ruther cut in. "A killer who gets life for murder."

"It would be more humane to take Lieutenant Nehalem out and shoot him," Veblen said bitterly.

"I'm sure he would rather have it that way. Life imprisonment in the Army means one thing—life imprisonment. No hope of freedom ever."

"I don't know the facts in the case, of course," Jessie admitted. "But I'm willing to bet anything that Greg Nehalem isn't guilty."

Ruther stiffened. "That's as good as callin' me a liar."

"No need to lose your temper," Veblen cautioned. "Personally, I haven't liked this case from the start. That's why Nehalem received a life sentence instead of the death penalty."

Ruther allowed a cold smile to touch his lips. "Pardon me, Major," he said suavely, trying to hide the thread of anger in his voice. Then, ignoring Jessie and Ki completely, he bowed to the major and left the room. Outside, he was joined by a blocky man who wore his dark hair long and was attired in greasy buckskins.

"Who's the gunhand?" Jessie asked Veblen as she watched the pair through the window.

"Hacho Chown. He was a witness, along with Ruther."

Halfway across the parade ground Quaid Ruther stopped and conversed for a moment with a young lieutenant. The two men shook hands, and Ruther climbed into the saddle of a gray gelding while Hacho Chown mounted another horse. They followed a lumbering freight wagon out the gate. Two men were on the seat of the freighter, and there was a saddle horse tied to the tailgate.

"Ruther seems friendly with one of your officers," Jessie observed.

"That was Lieutenant Wolcott. He also was a witness against Nehalem," the major replied. "There's been sort of bad blood between Wolcott and Nehalem anyway, on account Nehalem was commissioned from the ranks. That's unthinkable to an Academy man." Veblen sighed and shook his head. "Just before you arrived, in fact, Lieutenant Wolcott requested to be put in charge of the detail that will escort Nehalem to Fort Brown."

Jessie gave him a sharp glance, but the major did not expand on his statement, so she assumed that Wolcott's request had been granted, albeit reluctantly. She asked, "Would it be granting too much if we visited Nehalem?"

"Ordinarily I would not give permission," Veblen said, after a moment's hesitation. "But perhaps you—" He bit off the rest of the sentence, as if suddenly remembering that he was the commanding officer of this fort.

"Thank you, Major," Jessie said, after the officer had scribbled out a pass. "I've got a hunch it'll pay to hear Nehalem's side of this story."

Outside, she and Ki crossed the drill ground to the guardhouse. Here, Jessie showed her pass to the guard on the door and was allowed to enter the log building. The guardhouse at Fort Younger was one large room, with heavy barred windows and a grille that cut the room in half. In the forepart were stationed two guards, while in the cage area were grouped about a dozen prisoners. Jessie was not allowed in the cage, of course, so she had to stand by the bars while the guard shouted Nehalem's name.

15

When Jessie saw the tall, fair-haired young officer step forward, she hardly recognized him. No longer the lad she remembered, Greg Nehalem was now a full-grown, mature male in his late twenties, fine-featured, with an aquiline nose and prominent cheekbones. His auburn eyes were glittering with pent-up emotion—indicating he hadn't lost all of the explosive temper that had caused him trouble as a boy—but now bitterness shone in them, and there were deep lines in his face as well. He crossed the cage with dragging steps, but even though the stigma of murder rode his shoulders, he held his head high.

The lanterns had not been lighted yet, so it was nearly dark in the room. It wasn't until he was at the bars that the lieutenant let out a whoop of joy at sight of Jessie and Ki. He and Jessie clasped hands through the bars.

"It's been a long time, Greg," Jessie said soberly. "I surely never imagined you'd be in a tight like this."

At the reference to his sentence, Nehalem's face clouded and he gripped the bars so hard that his knuckles whitened against the metal. "You've heard the whole rotten mess then," he said in a voice heavy with defeat.

"But I haven't heard your story. Tell me what happened," Jessie said softly, so that the other prisoners would not overhear. "We're going to get you out of this."

"Jessie—and you, too, Ki—you know that an Army court-martial is as final as Judgment Day,"

Nehalem said with a shake of his head.

"Don't give up hope," Ki responded quickly, grasping the officer's arm. "You didn't get the noose, and that's something. Now we have more time to work."

Nehalem's jaw hardened. "The whole thing is so crazy that I can't believe it myself," he explained. "I'd been out on patrol getting a few head of cattle that had been run off by some Indians. I sent my men on into the fort, and I loitered along the way. I heard gunfire and immediately rode in the direction of the shots."

"What'd you find?" Jessie asked, when Nehalem hesitated.

His voice was grim when he answered. "I found an old Chinaman, dead, shot through the back. Nearby was his mule but nothing more.

"Where did Ruther come into this?"

"I was stooping over Fong Wah when Ruther and his two men jumped me. They covered me and accused me of killing the Chinese. I was arguing with them with Lieutenant Wolcott rode up. He and I had had some words the day before. Wolcott listened to Ruther's story, then took great delight in herding me back to the fort. I was put under arrest. When they searched my locker, they found a sack of Chinese coins. As Fong Wah had similar coins in a money belt, it was assumed that I had cached part of the loot on the post before having a chance of disposing of it."

"That's flimsy evidence."

"But evidence enough," Nehalem said bitterly.

"Somebody planted those coins. I had no defense. They even said that because I've been sparkin' a gal, I'd stolen the money so as to have a suitable start for married life."

"Anyone who really knew you would never think a thing like that," Ki declared.

"It was Dunton Wolcott's theory."

"Sure seems like he's got a lot to do with this," Jessie remarked after a moment of speculation. She was remembering how Ruther and Lieutenant Wolcott had shaken hands there on the parade ground. "I'm beginning to wonder what connection there is between Wolcott and this freighter, Quaid Ruther."

Nehalem shrugged. "Well, I grant there's more to the trouble than meets the eye," he went on. "You see, I knew Fong Wah. Got to know him and his son, Fong Lu, 'cause they run a laundry in Monument, the town where my gal lives. Fong Wah was one of the thousands of Orientals who built the Southern Pacific, Santa Fe, and other railroads through the Southwest, and then found themselves dumped when the lines were done. So he set up a laundry. Lately, times have been kind of rough, and lots of folks out of work like to blame the Chinese. I had to step in and save the laundry from some hot-tempered drunks who wanted to burn it down, and, well, we got to be good friends."

"Why would he have been coming here?" Ki asked.

"I've a feeling it was to see me," Nehalem answered. "Recently Fong Wah and his son have talked to me about Chinese disappearing—friends of theirs, and friends of friends. No one seems to know what's happened to them. Somehow they up and vanish, and their property gets taken over and sold on the open market. So far, the general public doesn't know, and quite likely if they did, they wouldn't care too awful much. Still, those responsible are evidently intent on keeping it a secret as long as possible. There's a chance, I reckon, that Fong Wah and his son found out something important, and they didn't have anyone other'n me that they felt they could go tell."

Jessie rubbed her chin and stared down at the board floor, still damp from its last scrubbing. "That might be worth following up on. We could go to Monument and find Fong Wah's son, see what he might know."

"If you do go thataway, would you do me a favor?"

"Sure, we will, Greg."

"Drop by the Bar-B-Bar just outside of town. It's owned by Oscar Bryce. Tell his daughter Adriane that . . . that I was accidently killed in a hunting accident."

"That's not being very fair to her, is it?"

"Fair!" Nehalem almost shouted. Then after a quick glance at the other prisoners, he dropped his voice. "I'll never get to Brownsville. I'm going to escape or— I'll never go there to rot."

"Don't lose your head," Jessie warned, recalling Nehalem's explosive temper.

"Anything's better than that hellhole stockade."

19

"Just don't give up hope," Ki reminded him.

"Hope?" Nehalem said with a tight laugh. "I leave at sunup for Fort Brown. And Lieutenant Wolcott has charge of the detail. I just heard the news from some of my"—he paused for a moment—"ex–brother officers."

"Greg, take heart. We'll try to locate Fong Lu," Jessie pledged, "and we'll go see Adriane Bryce."

"Give Adriane my message," Nehalem pleaded. "I'd druther she thinks me dead. She'll be free to find another man. If she knows I'm spending my life in prison, she may live in hope that someday I'll be free."

Even though Jessie realized the whole thing looked hopeless, she gave Nehalem a reassuring grin and, with Ki, left the guardhouse. Retrieving their traveling bags, they walked out of the main gate, down a short wagon trail to an unnamed sutler settlement below the fort. The settlement was a squalid hodgepodge of bleak saloons, dingy shops, plank shanties, tents, and sod hovels that looked as if the ground had merely swollen into shack-sized tumors. But it had what they were looking for—horses and supplies.

In charge of the small livery stable was a lean, red-necked hostler who kept up a running fire of gab as they inspected his stock. It took some searching, but among the cavvy of crowbait plugs, two capable and relatively young and healthy mounts were found—a hock-scarred moro gelding for Ki and a shaggy yet solid grulla mare for Jessie. Gear was carefully selected, a deal was struck, and they rode a couple of blocks to the settlement's general store. The inside was piled rafter-high, and it took a while to pick out supplies, ammunition, blankets, rifle scabbards, and Winchester '76 .45–75 carbines. Ki disliked guns as a rule, but out in the Texas wilds, a long-range, big-bore repeater was a practical need.

They headed out on the wagon road that would take them to the town of Monument, which lay a two-day's ride northeastward in the lower Colorado Valley, roughly a hundred miles southeast of Austin. About three hours after leaving Fort Younger, they came to a stage relay station, where they stopped to refresh and rest their horses. The corral held a relay team, but there was no one around but the stock boy—a furtive-eyed youth who seemed more than casually interested in their arrival. Striking up a rather forced conversation, as though to pump them for information, he chanced to remark that Ruther with his wagon had passed thataway.

"If we catch up with Ruther, let's give him wide berth," Jessie said as she and Ki hit saddle leather again. "At this point there's nothing to talk to him about, at least nothing that wouldn't rile him again."

Ki nodded, his keen onyx eyes taking in the sparse wooded slopes, still muddy from the previous night's storm. Instead of following the road now, he gave the signal to cut across the low ridge, which would save them several miles. His gelding's hoofs dug into the firm footing of the hillside, and soon they had reached the crest and could see a small valley that lay below.

It was only long habit of caution that caused Jessie to look back the way they had come. The relay station was only a tiny dot in the distance, but that was not what caught her eye. It was the column of black smoke that funneled skyward beside the building. Ki noticed it, too, and the skin over his cheekbones tightened as he pointed to the black puffs that broke off, then rose again.

"Smoke signals," he observed. "Not Indian, though."

"That stock boy at the station," Jessie said, eyes narrowing as she studied the smoke. "He's probably using a creosote fire and a blanket."

They both caught the smell of wood smoke in the breeze that blew against their cheeks.

"Maybe Ruther paid the kid to signal if we came by," Ki said, wheeling his horse and starting down the slant. "Keep your eyes peeled," he warned, "and your carbine handy."

They were on a rocky shelf, and the going was slippery because of the night's soaking rain. The skittish moro gelding lost its balance. Ki, superb horseman that he was, could do nothing but leave the saddle.

Jessie saw him go, rolling up in a tight ball to take up the shock. She whirled her grulla, made a grab for the moro's reins, but at that moment a bullet whistled past her ear and a rifle blasted off to her left. Catching a peripheral glimpse of powder smoke below, she spotted a heavy freight wagon pulled off the road in an oak grove, the team still in harness.

"Keep down!" she yelled at Ki as she spotted a

shadowy figure near the wagon's tailgate.

Ki had regained his feet and was now scrambling over the slippery shale, chasing after his panicky moro, which was plunging off into the stand of green oaks. Jessie feared that if she retreated, she would leave him unprotected. Therefore she drew her carbine and let the grulla have its head, attempting to guide the horse with her knees. She headed straight for the three guns that were now opening up from behind a cluster of boulders near the wagon. Carbine blazing, she put her horse at a zigzaggy run. A man's sombreroed head appeared above the rocks. The skulker was evidently confident he could pick off this reckless female rider.

Jessie fired instinctively. The man threw up his hands to fall back out of sight. Bullets from two other guns were singing their deadly song. Now Ki's carbine was added to the chorus of blasting weapons. But Ki was in plain sight. Jessie pressed her mouth with her knees, and the horse whirled in a tight circle. She galloped back the way she had come to cover Ki. It was treacherous going on the slippery shale, and any second she expected the horse's iron shoes to slide, but the horse kept its balance.

When Jessie reached Ki's side, she noticed the firing had ceased. There was the diminishing thud of hoofbeats, but she knew pursuit, under the circumstances, would be foolhardy.

"They've gone," Ki said, seeming unruffled at his narrow escape from death as he walked up, smoking carbine in hand.

Together they moved toward the boulders, where

they found a dead man sprawled on his back, a hole in his forehead.

"What do you think happened, Jessie?" Ki asked in a low voice, peering into the shadowy oak grove where they could see the freight wagon.

"No telling what their game is," she answered with a shrug. "You take a look over there while I search this one."

Without a word, Ki made his way through the brush.

The dead man was smooth-shaven, wearing a flannel shirt, black pants, and scuffed boots. His mouth was agape, his eyes staring at the sky. Swallowing thickly, Jessie went through his pockets with deft fingers. She found some coins, tobacco in an oilskin pouch, but nothing to identify the man or his mission.

Ki returned. "Nobody's about," he reported. "There're tracks of two riders going south. And I found this." He handed Jessie a piece of folded paper.

"That's a Chinese lottery ticket," Jessie exclaimed. "Unless I'm off the track, I'll bet Chinese were hauled in that wagon."

"There's nothing else in it to tell."

"Well, this ticket is the first piece of tangible evidence we can work on," she responded with a grim smile. "I wouldn't doubt that we've gotten Quaid Ruther worried. He fixed it with the stock boy to signal if we were on the trail. That gave him time to set the ambush."

"And he might be the one responsible for last night's guntrap," Ki allowed. "If, for instance, he

24

found out through that Lieutenant Wolcott that you'd written Major Veblen about Nehalem, perhaps he decided to do away with you before you could bring all of Starbuck in on this."

"Maybe . . . Maybe not . . . Time will tell, I imagine."

They buried the dead skulker there beside the road. Then Jessie mounted her grulla, and Ki went over to where he had caught his moro and tethered it to an oak. They rode to the freight wagon, unhitched the team, and turned the horses loose. There was no time to take them to a corral, and it would have been cruel to leave them tied up.

Then they started for Monument again, warier than ever.

★

Chapter 3

The following afternoon found Jessie and Ki in Monument. The sleepy little settlement reposed on the south bank of the Colorado River. It was vital that their horses have rest and a real feed, and besides, Jessie desired to locate Fong Wah's laundry and to get directions to the Bryce ranch. They first saw to their mounts' needs, and after a rubdown and a small drink for each horse, they left them in a corral behind the livery stable.

They walked up the awning-shaded way. A glance completely took in Monument. Main Street was the one real street, running on both sides of a plaza. There were three saloons, one of good size and advertising rooms for rent; a general store called Goldstein's; a blacksmith shop; the livery; a hardware store specializing in firearms and ammunitions; the laundry; and a few more shabby-fronted buildings. There was no sign of the law, but Jessie wasn't surprised; such a spot might boast a day constable and a night watchman, but for real law enforcement the town would have to depend on a sheriff from the county seat, some twenty miles away. There were a few saddle horses as well as farm wagons standing at the railings separating the sidewalks from the street. They indicated that Monument was the hub of a mixed community of ranches, farms, and homes nestling in the surrounding hill country—small operators, for since the Civil War the big outfits had moved or set up in the Trans-Pecos or far to the west, to avoid the crowding as farmers and crops growers came in.

The front door of the laundry was locked. Through the window, Jessie and Ki could not see anyone in the darkened interior, and they didn't see any sign of life when they checked around back, either. Hungry, thirsty, and tired, they strode to the largest of the saloons, the Palace Hotel and Club, where they ordered a meal and paid for rooms. From the desk clerk they learned that the laundry was only open three days a week, and today wasn't one of those days. Where the Fongs lived or went on their days off was a mystery; evidently nobody cared enough about the Chinese ever to bother wondering. The clerk did know the way to the Bar-B-Bar, though, and cheerfully gave detailed directions to the Bryce ranch.

Rather than wait around, Jessie decided they should ride out to the ranch. They saddled up and set out across low hills covered with brush and patches of woods. The Colorado cut through these with innumerable curves and indentations, and the wagon road meandered along the river valley, skirting natural obstructions above the high-water mark.

The Bar-B-Bar proved farther than they had

at first thought, and they were still some ways distant as the sun began to set. A warm wind rustled the summer foliage, and sudden gusts picked up dust from bare spots, depositing a coating of fine particles on whatever was handy. It cooled a bit with dusk, but it was still warm. They could hear the slow murmur of the Colorado to their right and occasionally see a stretch of the silvery water. As they moved upriver, they sighted here and there the small lights of homes, looking cozy and inviting.

An owl whistled eerily from the top of a scraggly oak. A disgruntled coyote answered with a querulous yipping. Somewhere a steer bawled thinly. The wind picked up, bringing patches of overcast. Over the looming hills hung a red and gibbous moon, now burning luridly, now obscured by the racing cloud rack. The stars vanished, then the moon. The night became black as pitch.

Jessie's grulla suddenly moved sharply forward, as if pricked. The next moment Jessie and Ki also heard what had attracted her horse's attention. Swelling out of the north was a pounding beat that swiftly grew louder.

"Horses," Ki said. "Lots of them and coming this way fast."

They pulled their mounts to a halt and sat listening.

"Whoever's hustling along," Jessie reckoned, "we better give them plenty of room."

Hastily they backed their mounts off the trail and into the fringe of brush that flanked it. The pounding of hoofbeats swelled to a rumbling roar

that drowned the moan of wind. They were directly ahead, now. Then they were surging past to the
accompaniment of the rumbling and bleating of
irritated cattle. Through a sudden break in the
clouds, moonlight illuminated the scene for a brief
moment. Jessie and Ki had a vision of tossing
horns, rolling eyes, and shaggy backs. The herd
was almost past where they sat their horses at
the edge of the trail. Riding hard on the heels of
the cattle, with loose reins and busy spurs, were
half a dozen horsemen who urged the lumbering
cows to greater efforts.

Ki heard a startled yell from their ranks. Instantly he shoved Jessie, unseating her, and then went
sideward himself out of his saddle. There was a
roar of gunfire, a crackling of bullets through the
branches over their heads. Their horses, snorting
explosively, lunged back into the brush.

Prone on the ground, Jessie yanked out her
pistol and sent a bunch of lead hissing toward
the unseen horsemen, who were now enveloped
in the blackness of the night. A yell of pain echoed
the shots. A slug or two whined past in answer.
But the roll of hoofbeats was undiminished. Swiftly they faded into the south.

"Nice little reception committee," she remarked
wrathfully, as she got to her feet and dusted herself off. "I think I winged one of them, going by his
yelping."

"The way they were shoving those cows along,"
Ki added, "I've a prime notion some spread hereabouts will be missing a herd of beefs in the morning."

Again the clouds parted for a moment, but revealed only a empty stretch of trail to the next bend. Jessie stared southward for a moment, then joined Ki in getting their horses from the brush. Mounting, they continued on, the trail flowing north with a slight bend to the west.

Presently, a puff of west wind blew dust into Ki's eyes, and he turned his chin down and shook his head. Cleaning his eyes of particles, he looked ahead once again, sighting lighted windows some distance on. The road hugged an undercut cliff, and both he and Jessie were against the darkness here. It was then that Jessie's grulla shivered and slowed without any knee pressure, followed by Ki's more sniffing softly as though to give warning.

"Something's spooking them again," Jessie said.

Immediately Ki drew up and sat his saddle with ear cocked. Jessie, too, waited, as patient as Fate. The animal senses of their mounts were keener than any human's could be, and even though there was no thunderous noise as there had been with the passing herd, some scent had reached the horses' flared nostrils, brought on the wind.

At last they were rewarded as they caught the sounds of splashing from the river, somewhere upstream.

"Riders," Ki murmured, "crossing the Colorado."

They moved on a bit, hunting a possible niche in the cliff into which to retire in case the riders came their way. Again they pulled up, pressing back and freezing. The horsemen were coming up the slope onto the road, and they saw a cigarette glow ruby red in a man's mouth as the smoker dragged on it. Voices reached them.

"Douse that quirly and keep shut," an irritated command was snapped out. "You want 'em to savvy you're comin'?"

The cigarette was doused after a final inhalation. The dark figures swung up the river road away from Jessie and Ki, who guessed their number to be about a dozen or so. Allowing the riders a lead, they followed in the dust kicked up by the trotting horses until the riders reined in and dismounted some distance out from a lighted house. Two holders were left with the horses to keep them quiet as the others started quietly toward the dwelling.

Ground-reining their horses in the shadow of a brush clump, Jessie and Ki circled the spot where the riders' horses restlessly pawed and sniffed, and overheard the low talk of the holders. It was too dark to see much of the surroundings, but they could make out that the area about the house and outbuildings was cleared, fringed by patches of woods and brush. The stealthy attackers used this cover as they crept forward.

Listening intently, Jessie and Ki could hear men moving in a small grove of trees to their left. They could not see the men at all now, and the faint noises seemed thin for so many, so they froze behind a jutting tongue of rock, a great boulder half-buried in the earth. The progress of someone in the woods was checked and then resumed. They caught a few words:

"The gal's got a sentry on the porch, Hacho," a

man was reporting. "I seen his gun barrel when he shifted."

Jessie whispered to Ki: "The main bunch must've waited while a scout went to the edge of the woods to spy on the house."

Ki nodded, whispering back: "And I bet 'Hacho' is Hacho Chown, who works for Quaid Ruther. Looks like he's got himself a little moonlighting job."

Another speaker's voice reached their ears, and they thought it was the same gruff one that had cautioned the riders on the road. "Gimme the new Sharps. I'm going to crawl over to that rock and lie there and see what I can hit. If they got a guard out, there's no chance of rushin' in, but maybe I can pick off Moss or one of the waddies. You boys stick here and keep it quiet. Cover me."

Jessie and Ki, lying squeezed against the opposite side of the rock, could hear the creeping enemy crossing from the woods to the boulder. Motioning for Jessie to stay absolutely still, Ki started easing his way around to where he could intercept the man. Before he could get ready, the man stopped on the near edge of the rock and set himself there. Ki sought to control his breathing. It seemed to him that it must be extra loud, but he could not hear the fellow on the other side, except when the latter moved. By raising his eyes, Ki could see the side windows; through one showed an oil lamp burning on the table, and a woman's figure passed between the window and light. Then a man went by the same window.

Ki heard the throaty *cluch-cluck* of the cocking

33

Sharps. A man again was silhouetted against that light now and paused at the table to pick up something, a newspaper or magazine. This made him a sitting duck target for an expert marksman. Springing, Ki vaulted the boulder and landed with both feet in the small of the back of the prostrate bushwhacker. The Sharps went off with a deafening roar and glass tinkled. A woman inside the house screamed shrilly in terror, and a man began cursing.

Ki had wrecked the drygulcher's aim, but he quickly found that he had tackled a wildcat—a wildcat he instantly recognized as Hacho Chown. Pivoting, Chown slashed at Ki with the heavy rifle barrel and nearly cracked Ki's left forearm. Ki slipped his vise grip to the warm steel of the barrel and with a wrench ripped the Sharps away and flung it aside. But in this moment Chown got to his knees and slugged him in the solar plexus with a pile-driver punch.

It was a paralyzing blow, and Ki nearly lost his life as Chown whipped out a revolver and leveled it point-blank. Desperate, Ki threw himself forward. The revolver blasted in his ear, and he felt the burn of flashing powder against his cheek. The bullet missed him by a breath, and with all his skill, Ki slid a hand from the gun wrist and closed his fingers on the cylinder. The revolver could not be fired again while he held on. Simultaneously he brought up a knee and Chown grunted in pain. Ki's ears still rang with the explosion of the gun, and only dimly was he aware of yells and calls from both the house and the woods where Chown

34

had left his men. Boring in, Ki bent Chown's arm and forced him to release the revolver. Chown turned so his bone would not be snapped by the pressure, then suddenly fell back, carrying Ki with him. Ki landed on top but was slugged in the nose with such force that his eyes watered.

"Hacho! Hacho! What's wrong? Come on!"

A gunshot banged from the direction of the house as the sentry let one go at the noises and the spot where he had seen the Sharps flame. A bullet whizzed over Ki and Hacho as they struggled on the sandy dirt. Hacho was as slippery as a greased pig, and he could take a lot of punishment. He never quit struggling, and he began to shout, "This way, boys! Over here!"

Ki was aware of a rush from the woods. The riders who had come here with Hacho were entering the fight. It would mean death. He was sure Hacho had another gun in his holsters, and he wanted to disable the man enough so that Hacho could not kill him when he turned. Gripping Hacho's shirt, he picked him up off the earth and started to hurl him away. But the shirtfront was rotted and ripped in Ki's grip. The whip of it sent Hacho reeling toward his followers, who had almost reached him, but dared not fire into the melee, for fear of killing their leader.

The sudden release of Hacho's weight sent Ki staggering back, and his heels caught on a low rock shelf. He fell back and brushed against the sharp side of the boulder, still unconsciously holding most of Hacho's shirtfront in his hand. Dark figures were dashing at him from the woods. Hacho was rolling

35

over and over toward the oncoming men and yelling to them at the top of his lungs:

"Kill him! Kill the bastard o'er there!"

Revolvers blared, and lead spattered against the stone. Ki flipped himself around and scrabbled over the top of the boulder, dropping the piece of shirt he'd been gripping. Jessie, pistol in hand, took aim at Hacho and would have shot him then and there, but the others suddenly came swarming around their chief. Hacho was frantically trying to tell them what had occurred and pointing at the boulder. Jessie bobbed up to shoot, and her bullets sent them streaking back into the woods, Hacho with them. But one man threw up his hands and crashed with a howl before he could reach shelter.

Jessie dusted the brush, her lead spaced in the trees. She tried to judge where they were by the cracklings made as they retreated toward their horses, but gunfire opened behind her. Men from the house had circled, and the light in the house had been put out. A bullet smacked into the rock near Ki, sent by the very men he and Jessie had come to help. They could not distinguish friend from foe in the night and were alarmed by the attempted ambush.

"Hold it!" Jessie called, edging to the side of the rock.

A hard and determined voice answered, "Whozzat?"

"Friends!"

"Yeah? Do frien's shoot an hombre through the window?"

There was no more shooting from the woods.

Hacho and his men had fled except for the silent figure lying facedown a few yards from the trees.

"We didn't fire that shot," Jessie argued. "Listen and you'll hear the ambushers riding off. We stopped them from shooting you."

There was a silence. Jessie and Ki, crouched by the boulder, could hear men all around them, each with a bead on them. The beat of retreating hoofs helped win the argument for them.

"If you're frien's, come out with your hands reachin'!" another voice called. "Steady, now!"

They stood up and raised their hands, slowly walking into the open space. They had made it about twenty paces when the hard voice ordered:

"Now stop and let's have a look at y'all."

They complied. A man rose from behind them and came carefully closer, a carbine leveled and cocked. Jessie could see him out of the corner of her eye, a husky, hard-featured, saddle-worn cowhand. A shorter, older waddie, with a tobacco cud thrusting out one leathery cheek, jumped up at Ki's left and bored in, covering him.

The first man gingerly lifted Jessie's pistol from her holster. The second man yelled, "This'un ain't armed, Moss!" then squinted querulously at Ki. "Is yuh?"

"You're losing time," Jessie said. "Your ambushers are way off by now."

"What's it to you?" a third man demanded, approaching out of the darkness. He was a burly old man with white Dunrearie whiskers furring his weathered face. "How come you were with them, anyhow?"

"We weren't *with* them," Jessie replied. "We were heading for the Bryce Bar-B-Bar ranch, bumped into a dozen drygulchers and trailed them here. Ki, here, had a scrap with one who tried for you from this rock when you showed in front of the lamp."

"The Bar-B-Bar, eh? Wal, you made it, lady. This here is the Bryce spread, and I'm Moss, foreman. These're a coupla my crew, Rob"—he indicated the first man—"and Hank." He indicated the man covering Ki. "Wal, come on into the house and and we'll talk this over."

"Better check up outside first," Jessie advised. "I shot one of them when they ran for the woods."

"Rob, fetch a lantern!" Moss ordered.

As Rob padded toward the barn, a woman's voice called from the house: "Moss! Moss, are you all right?"

"Yeah, we're fine!" Moss answered. "We'll be in in a jiffy, Miss Adriane."

Rob returned with a lighted bull's-eye lantern, which he handed to Moss. Holding it high, the foreman walked with Jessie and Ki toward the body, saying, "These are the same gunslingers, I'm convinced, that killed an old friend and neighbor of Mist' Bryce's, named Walter Dunham. This's the second time they've tried for us, not countin' once when we found Dunham's corpse in the hills and they chased us home. They were here last week, but we beat 'em off."

Reaching the body, Ki rolled it over. "Never seen him afore," Moss declared, and the two hands agreed.

Hank suggested, "I'll get a shovel, Boss, and we'll bury this lobo where he lies."

Moss nodded, turning to Jessie and Ki. "I'll tell you all we savvy. But first let's go inside and have a drink—er, of coffee." He carried the lantern as they went back toward the house, and as they passed close to the rock where Ki had fought Hacho, the circle of light showed the dark piece of shirt that Ki had ripped from him.

"Wait a minute, Moss," Ki said. "Fetch the light closer."

He stopped and picked up the sweated cloth. The flap of the breast pocket was open as the button had been pulled from its moorings, and Ki glimpsed edges of a sheet of white paper sticking out. He drew it forth and unfolded it, holding it to the lantern so he and Jessie could see what it was. Moss, too, bent close to read the words inscribed on the paper. In round, even handwriting, each letter formed with scrupulous care, was a list of names, headed by that of Dunham. A line had been drawn through Dunham's name. The second on the list was Bryce.

"You recognize who all these folks are?" Jessie asked Moss.

"Some. Dunham is dead. Bryce is next, us no doubt included. The third is John Phelps, a neighborin' rancher with a spread runnin' back from the valley. Lives there with his wife and four kids. Fourth is Sam Oliphant, up the line from us. He's owner of a small ranch. All decent folk, all livin' within fifteen miles of here in the hills."

They went on to the house as Jessie pocketed the strange list. She was taking a graver and graver view of it as she mulled it over in her mind. Walter Dunham was already dead. They had tried for Oscar Bryce, and evidently were willing to kill Bryce's daughter and crew in the bargain.

A girl standing in front of the porch hurried up to them. "What is it? Those raiders again?"

"Yes, Miss Adriane," Moss answered. "They've gone now."

Moss led the way inside and struck a match. It had been Moss between the lamp and window, and the bullet sent by Hacho had missed by two feet, smashing the pane of glass and going high, thanks to Ki's action. As Moss lit the table lamp, the girl turned to face Jessie and Ki, saying, "I'm Adriane Bryce. Welcome to the Bar-B-Bar ranch."

Jessie introduced herself and Ki, who swept off his hat and bowed. The powder-blue calico dress Adriane was wearing could not hide the curvaceousness of her figure, and such golden hair and liquid amber eyes as hers would have cast a spell over any man. Ki was no exception, and his head to toe to head glance was frankly admiring.

"I'll see to it your horses are tended," Moss offered, then looked at the girl. "I've a notion your guests could stand a cup or two of coffee, Miss Adriane."

"Why, of course. The kitchen is out this way," she said to them, taking the lamp from the table. She led them into a big roomy kitchen, where she busied herself stoking the cookstove fire and

40

setting on a fresh pot of coffee. "I'm sorry about how you were first greeted, but we've had trouble, and never know what to expect. We're a little suspicious of strangers."

Jessie pursed her lips, thinking that with Moss gone and the two crewmen out burying the body, this was a good a time as any to broach a delicate subject. "We're not precisely strangers, Adriane. We're friends of Greg Nehalem."

A faint flush stained the girl's cheeks, and a smile quirked the corners of her mouth as she began to talk excitedly of Nehalem, wondering how he was, if he were coming soon to Monument.

"This is going to be hard, Adriane, but I want you to know it isn't as bad as it sounds," Jessie said seriously. And as she talked, telling of Nehalem's trial and subsequent sentence, she wondered at her own rashness in projecting a note of optimism.

The color had drained from Adriane Bryce's cheeks, and now she turned quickly to hide the tears that had suddenly come to her dark eyes.

"He didn't want you to know," Jessie said reassuringly, patting her slender shoulder in a gesture of sympathy. "I figure we can get him free, just as soon as we get to the bottom and line up the facts."

Adriane faced her again. "I'm glad that Greg has friends like you and Ki," she said in a low voice. "You've given me courage. On top of the attacks and . . . and my father gone, I don't know whether I could carry on."

"Gone? Oscar Bryce has died?"

Adriane shook her head. "He's disappeared."

"Texas is a big state. Perhaps he's just—"

"I'm afraid he's in trouble," Adriane said. "If you ever get up into the back hill country, look for him. We've been strapped for money, so he took an extra job freighting for a man named Quaid Ruther."

Jessie's nerves tensed at this information. She didn't tell her of Ruther's connection with Nehalem, figuring Adriane had enough to worry about.

"I've planned to leave tomorrow for White Mule," Adriane said. "That was the last place Dad wrote from."

Jessie stared at the girl after this rather startling announcement, at a loss as to just what to say. Before she could speak, a chatter of excited voices sounded outside, followed by steps running swiftly toward the kitchen door. Adriane hurried to the door and flung it open.

Moss and another elderly waddie entered, supporting between them a young cowhand who reeled drunkenly on dragging feet. His eyes were wild, his face pale and haggard. One cheek was crusted with dried blood that had oozed from a ragged furrow just above his left eyebrow.

"Chuck!" Adriane gasped. "What happened?"

"Plugged," the cowhand mumbled. "Knocked me off my hoss and down into the brush. Reckon the coyotes figgered I was done for. Anyhow, they didn't come to finish me. Managed to catch my hoss and hang on till I got here."

"Where's Elmore?" the girl asked anxiously.

"Dead. Drilled dead center. They got the herd."

"Who did it?"

"How'n thunderation would I know?" Chuck complained. "I heard hosses comin' out of the brush, then the whole world blew up inside my head. When I come to, I found Elmore cashed in. The herd was gone."

As Moss was about to voice a question of his own, Jessie interrupted. "First chore is to look after this fellow. Set him down in that chair. Get some rags and hot water. That head of his needs attention." Swiftly, efficiently, she cleansed the wound. She probed the skull beneath with sensitive fingers and decided that there was no fracture. "Hit you a nasty lick, but you'll be all right as soon as the headache wears off," she told the puncher. "You say you didn't see any of the rustlers?"

The cowhand wearily shook his head. "Didn't see nothin'."

"I suspect Ki and I did," Jessie suddenly remarked.

The others gave her startled looks.

Briefly she recounted what had happened on the trail south of the ranch.

"That would be our herd, okay," Moss declared. "Headin' for environs south, like Mexico. How many hellions did you say there was?"

"About six, I'd say," Jessie told him. "They were moving the cows along almighty fast. Too fast to make sense, I'd say."

"How's that?"

"As you know, cows can soon be run off their feet," Jessie explained. "A tuckered herd could

43

never make it across the desert flats into Mexico. Those rustlers must've known that they didn't have anything to worry about, that there wasn't a chance of anybody being on their tail. They evidently figured they'd killed both nighthawks, and that it would be way past morning before anybody found out what had happened. Why all their hurry, then?"

"The owlhoot sort is always scared of something" was Moss's explanation.

Jessie did not comment further, but finished bandaging the wounded puncher's head.

"You'd better get to bed, Chuck," Adriane told her crewman. "And Moss, you and Jasper ride out in the morning and bring in poor Elmore's body."

Ki spoke up then: "I'm thinking you oughtn't to waste any time in warning your friends and neighbors listed on that paper we found. In my opinion every rancher on it will be killed, and likely their families and crew as well."

Adriane gasped, and Moss stiffened, his thick brows drawing together. "By Jupe you're right, Ki! Come to think of it, that list has to mean what you say. They aim to clean out these hills."

"Why?" Jessie asked.

Moss shrugged. "You got me there. Dunham's place ain't worth fifty cents an acre, and the other spreads are far from gold mines, either."

Jessie thought it over, but as yet she could not guess the reason for Hacho's attack on the inhabitants of this region. "I'm in favor of getting those warnings out tonight, if at all possible," she said grimly. "When we were on our way here we saw the raiders crossing the river a few miles back toward Monument. Suppose they returned that way? Whose place would it bring them closest to?"

"John Phelps's farm," Adriane answered.

"They were very riled at what happened. They're apt to lash out blind and take out their rage on whoever is near. Their leader has lost the list, but he'll likely remember some of the names on it. Phelps comes after yours."

Moss agreed. "But I dasn't leave Miss Adriane here unguarded, though," he objected.

"Tell us how to reach Phelps's and we'll go there ourselves," Jessie said. "Send your crew with notes to warn the others. You stick here with Adriane and the wounded puncher, Chuck, and watch your home."

★

Chapter 4

Adriane gave Jessie a brief note to John Phelps.
Then, with Ki, Jessie left Adriane busy writing
further warnings to the people named on the list,
and went out to collect their horses. Mounting,
they set out for the Phelps spread, alert and
ready for anything, but only the moon-bathed
hills loomed before them as they climbed from
the valley into the surrounding hills. Save for the
sounds of nature, the land seemed peaceful and
deserted. Eventually, after about an hour's ride,
they sighted the lights of a house, set well back
from the river.

"That should be it," Jessie said.

Dismounting out of the circle of light, they
scouted closer. They could see no horses, and as
they strained their ears to listen, they caught the
sound of a woman in the house sobbing, sobbing
with heartbroken despair.

They knew then what must have happened.
They knocked on the front door, and the crying
was checked. There was a silence and then a
frightened voice gasped, "Who is it?"

"Friends," Jessie replied gently. "Adriane Bryce

sent us to warn you, but I'm afraid we're too late."

After a time, the bolt was pulled back and the door opened. They looked down at a small woman with black hair drawn tightly back from her pallid face. Her eyes were red from weeping, and when they glanced past her, they saw a man lying on the couch.

It was difficult for her to talk. "My husband," she whispered. "Dead!" She was evidently suffering from shock.

"Mama!" a child called. "Who's there?"

"Hush, Gary, it's all right," she soothed, trying to keep the anguish and fright from her voice as she reassured the boy.

Fury burned in Jessie. Seeing the stricken family who had lost husband and father made Ki, too, grind his teeth in baffled anger. Beaten away at Bryce's, Hacho and his bunch had struck Phelps and murdered.

Mrs. Phelps soon made it clear that she had no intention of leaving her husband's body during the night. However, she promised that she would come with her children to the Bryce ranch after the burial, which would take place the next day.

Unable to be of further service, Jessie and Ki rode with heavy hearts back to the Bar-B-Bar. As they turned from the road into the ranch lane, Moss reared from the brush, challenging them. Then, recognizing them, he reported that the wounded cowhand, Chuck, was on guard way down by the river, in case the raiders decided to sneak attack thataway; that the rest of the crew was still out spreading the warning; and that so

48

far all had remained quiet. Leaving him cussing over the news about Phelps, Jessie and Ki rode on down the lane to the ranch house. Adriane was still up, fretful. Crying softly at hearing that Phelps had been killed, she showed them to their guest rooms, and they all retired . . .

Sometime later, Ki awoke with the need to take a piss. In just his shirt and jeans, he quietly padded outside and across the yard to the outhouse, a small but powerful two-holer concealed by tall brush.

Stepping from the outhouse to return, he halted at the door, hearing a faint scratching noise from beyond the brush. When it ceased a moment later, he chalked it up to a foraging rodent, and hastened on from the outhouse. Following the footpath that wound through the brush, he cleared the last turn and reached the yard at a quickening pace—

And collided with Adriane, who was rushing from the brushy fringe, clad only in a peignoir. He almost brained her before recognizing who it was.

"Don't shoot!" she gasped.

"I'm not armed."

"Well, you never can be too sure about that." She snuggled up against him, like a cat seeking affection, her voice faltering. "I . . . I hoped it was you. I feel so alone and scared."

"You got Moss and Chuck standing sentry."

"That's not the same." Her chin trembled, a portent of tears. "You must think me such a sissy."

"No, and don't you think it. Everyone lets their

hair down now and then, and after all you've suffered, nobody deserves to more than you."

"Not me. I won't buckle," she insisted, eyes misty. "Damn, I wish I was a man."

"If you were," Ki said, growing chary, "a lot of other men would be sorely upset."

"Not a lot; that's mean of you." She pressed her face against his chest. Ki heard her sob, and even while calling himself a sucker, he placed an arm around and patted her shoulder to comfort her. He conjured up things to say that might dampen her creeping ardor, but she kissed him before he could open his mouth. Responding, growing aroused, he was also growing worried about playing her game. He wondered how far she'd tease, how far was *too* far, and he didn't want to hurt her any more than she was hurt already.

"Adriane, you don't have to—"

"I know." She laid her hands on his chest, palms flat, fingers kneading. "I want to."

"I wouldn't mind, either, but what about Greg Nehalem?"

"I'd rather not discuss him. Besides, Greg isn't here now; you are." She pressed her body against him, her arm circling his back and clinging as she kissed him again for a long, burning moment. Ki kissed back enthusiastically, feeling her lips clinging hungrily, her breasts mashing against his chest, her hands shifting to rub along his hips.

They broke for air, but she continued to grip intimately. "We can't stay here."

Ki nodded. Moss or Chuck might come patroling by, or the whole damn crew could show up anytime

50

and see them. And if they did, he'd a hunch it'd cause one hell of a big brouhaha hereabouts. "But where?"

Adriane was barefooted, and she was quick on her toes in more ways than one. Pulling Ki by the hand, she ran across the yard and darted into a grove that separated the yard from the riverbank. The ground was typical summer hardpan, rougher than a cob, and as Ki followed along, he wondered if Adriane had a penchant for stand-up sexing.

They continued, threading their way through the tangle of rocks, brush, and trees, until they reached a clump of boulders. As they moved between the boulders, Ki saw that the screening rock encircled a small patch of grass, the ground dry and yet getting enough water seepage from the river to sustain the greenery.

Adriane then showed him a different nature lesson. She backed him up against one of the boulders, squeezing so close to him that he could feel the hotly beating pulse of her. They began kissing again, and as often as Ki kissed her, Adriane paid back the kisses, with wanton interest—until finally she drew away and stood in front of him. Humming provocatively, she pulled her peignoir over her head, her pert breasts swaying gracefully as she tossed her gown high, letting it float to the grass.

Buckass naked, she cuddled closer. "What's keeping you?" she purred, grabbing Ki's rope belt and tugging.

Ki felt the tug all the way down through his taut loins. Adriane crushed her body to his, kissing him

51

with hot, moist urgency. She helped him out of his shirt, and then, kneeling, she stripped him of his jeans, baring him to the cool night air. Still crouching, she leaned forward and gave a light kiss to the tip of his involuntarily swelling erection, her tongue starting to move caressingly over its blunt, burgeoning crown. Ki shivered reflexively, knowing he should put a halt to her, yet caught up in the impulse of the moment. Adriane was impish and fresh, but she was hot, as hot as the tantalizing feel of her lips and tongue guiding his now-rigid manhood into her widening mouth.

Her teeth scraped along his aching shaft as she tightened her lips and began a tentative sucking motion. Her hands stroked him while she bobbed her mouth back and forth, swallowing continuously, absorbing more of his throbbing erection into her mouth. Ki resisted the sensations flooding his loins, gritting his teeth in an attempt to hold himself back . . . until without warning, she released his shaft and rubbed its swollen head against her nose.

"The taste simply drives me wild," she murmured.

He drew her straight up against him, then back down in an embrace to lie stretched out on the grass. His hands moved compulsively, spreading tenderly across her flat stomach and up over her nubile breasts. He could feel her trembling from his touch, and warmth flowed through him, warmth as downy as the texture of her skin. Adriane shuddered and gripped him by the waist, pulling him over her, urging his hand to slide between her legs and upward along her sleek inner thighs. Her hips slackened, widening to allow him access while she kept murmuring in a low, passionate voice, "Make it good, Ki. Fill me up, make it good . . ."

What was made was a hard, quick union. Ki lunged deep into her in sheer lust. Adriane moaned in her eagerness and pushed her pelvis upward in an arc, to devour him, deep and hot, sliding into her belly. Faint cries of animal pleasure rose from her throat, her face contorting with desire, her mouth moving hungrily, her thighs rhythmically squeezing around Ki's pumping flesh. They were no longer aware of anything but the incredible sensations of the moment. Ki quickened his thrusts, searing and pulsating, and the exquisite agony of approaching orgasm caused Adriane to squirm beneath him.

"Ohhh . . . ," she cried, humping faster and faster against him. Ki was aware only of the magnificent pressure building inside him, and of the friction of their bodies as they heaved against each other. He climaxed so violently that for an instant he was unaware that Adriane, too, was coming, squeezing her inner muscles in tempo with his pulsing ejections. She circled her legs around him, locking her ankles, bucking upward with her hips, thighs, and buttocks, and claimed the last drops of joy there between her legs.

Slowly Ki settled down over her soft, warm body. He lay, crushing her breasts and belly with his weight, until his immediate satiation began to wane. He rolled from her then, and gently stroked her quivering breasts.

She smiled at him with lazy, satisfied eyes.

"You'll get me going again."

"Great, but not now. We should be getting back."

" 'Great, but not now.' In a minute, Ki—let me enjoy another minute. Oh, and how I wish . . ."

"Wish."

"There's a madness going on in these hills. A madness that's taken Mr. Dunham and Mr. Phelps now, and maybe has taken my father, and's threatening to take Greg, too. I wish I could stop the madness, but I can't. I must do what I can, make the best of the life I have." She curled tight against him, smiling wanly and stroking him with affectionate fingers. "I must make the best of you," she purred throatily, and Ki could feel the blood stirring in his loins again. "And there are many minutes left, Ki, there's plenty of time."

Good God, Ki thought dizzily, when a woman is offering, a man will somehow rise to the occasion. Even if it kills him . . .

Early the next day, Jessica walked from her second-floor guest room to the stairs, where she found Ki standing on the landing, resting against the balustrade as if for support, a numb expression on his face.

"Morning," she greeted. "Tired?"

Ki regarded her blearily.

"Serves you right. I know you like to keep in shape, but must you go out exercising when everyone else is trying to sleep?"

"Special nocturnal training," Ki replied, stifling a yawn. "Very important for conditioning reflexes in the dark, and it's particularily helpful for improving night vision."

54

"You mean for growing bags under your eyes," Jessie retorted with a wry smile, moving past him to descend the stairs. Ki slowly followed, a slight shuffle to his walk. In the kitchen, they joined Adriane for a savory breakfast of ham and eggs, coffee, and rolls. If Jessie noticed that Adriane's usually svelte grace was hampered by a rather stiff, bowlegged gait, she didn't mention it.

Together they saddled up and set out for the Phelps place. Moss accompanied them, driving the ranch wagon to bring Mrs. Phelps and the children back after the funeral. Arriving early, they pitched in to help the widow and her sister straighten things up, and greet neighbors as they came in wagons or on horseback and the preacher when he finally showed up from town.

All the men were curious about the grim warning sent them by Adriane, as was natural. While waiting for the services to begin, she talked with all of them, introducing Jessie and Ki to Duke Ulman, a rancher, Charlie Sutton, a farmer, and Sam Oliphant, who owned a little spread up the river from the Bar-B-Bar. Oliphant, a big breezy man of forty, had a wife and children and five hired cowhands. Van Lewis was another whose name was on the death list now in Jessie's pocket. Lewis was a former Confederate soldier and owned a farm north of Phelps's, up in the hill country. He was short and slim, dark of features, with expressive black eyes. Mark Ellsworth, still another of the intended victims, had a cabin downriver near Monument; he had a small income, raised crops in season, and had a few cows and chickens to cke

55

out a living for his growing family.

The names on the list resolved thus into living people with the hopes and fears of humanity, men on whom women and children depended for life itself. Jessie and Ki gauged them and liked them. They had faults and foibles, but so did all people.

Later that afternoon, when the remains of John Phelps had been given proper burial, Jessie and Ki met stout "Pop" Murphy, whose Irish brogue was amusing to hear and whose good nature never deserted him.

"Pop's the champion of the hills," Adriane explained, smiling. "He's got more kids than anybody else. How many is it, Pop—fourteen or fifteen?"

Murphy grinned, too. "Ah, I lose count of the rascals meself." He also had had a warning from Adriane, for his name was on the death list. And, like the others, he sought to understand what was going on.

"We're not sure," Adriane replied. "Best we can figure is that this gang wishes to clean us all out of the hills."

"But why?"

"That's a real mystery," Jessie answered. And it was, too, although she and Ki knew some facts that so far they had not divulged—that the gang had been led by Hacho Chown, that Chown worked for Quaid Ruther, that they had both helped send Greg Nehalem to prison, and that the matter of kidnapped or murdered Chinese seemed somehow involved as well—well, that just made it all the more a mystery. Until she had a better notion of if and how these perplexing pieces fit together, Jessie preferred to stay mum. "Have you seen any strangers or odd happenings in the hills?"

Frowning, Pop Murphy shook his head. So did the other men. Suddenly Sam Oliphant snapped his fingers and spoke up: "Wait a jiffy! One time I was huntin' a few of my cows in the hills. I run onto an hombre in black leather and he had a Spanish-lookin' feller with him. I spoke to 'em, asked if they'd seen my cattle. They said no. I told my name and asked theirs, and this swell with the beard says his was Pomgranite or somethin' like it. I didn't get it clear. The Spanish one stared at me without sayin' a word till it gave me the creeps. I was glad to be shut of 'em."

"How long ago was this?" Jessie asked.

Oliphant considered. "I'd say three, four months back."

Again Jessie thought: *But why?* Glancing around, she saw that most of the people were preparing to return to their homes. Mrs. Phelps and her four children, aged two to nine, would go to the Bryce ranch, although they had a dozen offers of hospitality, accompanied by Adriane and several of their concerned neighbors. Turning to Ki, Jessie said, "I think everything's under control here. Let's ride into Monument and see if we can find Fong Lu."

Light of day was fading when Jessie and Ki sighted the settlement, and it was growing darker as they rode down Main Street. Lamps had come on, and the Palace Hotel and Club was brightly lighted. The smell of supper cooking was in the

57

warm air. Men and women were about, and horses and teams stood in the gutters.

Jessie and Ki reined up in front of the Chinese laundry, only to find it dark and deserted again. "Too late," Jessie said. "I guess it already closed for the day."

"Or perhaps it never opened at all," Ki pointed out.

Jiggering their horses moving again, they headed on toward the hotel. Out of habit, they kept their eyes peeled as they rode along the street, which was livening a bit with the approach of evening. It was Ki who noticed the man first, and he pointed him out to Jessie.

"Look there, that guy going in the saloon."

The man was large, Jessie saw, wearing a leather jacket and a brown Stetson. "Quaid Ruther! Looks like he has a couple of his teamsters along with him."

"No sign of Hacho, though."

"Keep back," Jessie warned. "Let them get inside. And then let's go see what we can see."

"Well, assuming they hit the barroom, I'll go see what's to see."

Jessie nodded reticently, knowing she couldn't go in herself; the Palace was typical in that ladies could go there to sleep, eat, but not to drink, not without causing a scandal. In the shadows of the long wooden awning over the sidewalk, they quietly dismounted, then entered the lobby. Raucous noise rolled in eddies from the adjoining saloon, there being no partition between the lobby and the bar area. The two were, in fact, one large room divided only by their furnishings—and by popularity, the saloon crowded with thirsty drinkers, keeping three bartenders busy at the ornate, mirror-blazing bar.

The two riders who had entered with Quaid Ruther were halfway down the line and had shouldered to the counter. They were banging with their fists and calling for drinks. But neither Jessie nor Ki could see Ruther himself.

Sitting down on a sofa in the lobby, Jessie waited and watched Ki as he sauntered into the saloon. He was spotted by Ruther's men, and they began to scowl as they assumed a ready attitude. Both wore low-slung revolvers, and they were bearded, dirty, and tough in aspect. The way they dog-eyed Ki made Jessie wonder if perhaps they recognized him from the raid last night. Ki feigned not to notice as he elbowed a place at the bar and ordered a whiskey.

From her vantage, Jessie could also watch the comings and goings in the lobby. On the far side of the reception desk, a wooden staircase led to the floor above; behind the desk, a callow desk clerk surreptitiously ogled Jessie; and on the desk counter, a large ledger used as the hotel register lay open. Ki was halfway through his slow drink before Quaid Ruther came down the stairs and crossed the lobby, pausing with a startled expression when he caught sight of Jessie. Discombobulated, he then swept the saloon with a swift glance, spotted Ki, and headed toward the rear of the bar.

When Ruther raised a hand to signal the bartender, it looked to Jessie as though he were waving a cured ham. "That hand of his never wrote the fine letters on my list," she thought. "If he can scrawl he's lucky."

Now another man man came downstairs—a slim, swarthy, Spanish-looking man in a plain black suit and derby hat. Expressionless, without the slightest acknowledgment of anyone including the clerk, he carried two heavy valises across the lobby and out the front door. Through the window, Jessie could see him turn left and head in the direction of the livery stable.

A few minutes later, a third man descended to the lobby, a man entirely different from Ruther and the Spaniard in appearance. In his fifties, big of bone and flesh, the man wore a round-cut sack suit, a raw-edged fedora, and blucher-style calf boots. His jowled, double-chinned face sported a close-trimmed gray mustache and goatee, and its flesh had an unhealthy sallow cast, as did his pudgy hands, on the right pinky of which sparkled a fat diamond ring. He, too, stopped in the lobby, and though he stared straight at Ruther, no sign of recognition passed between them.

Drawn by the puzzle of it all, Jessie moved closer, feigning to be hunting a seat nearer the reception desk. The man had reached the desk, his face seamed with a smile as he nodded to the clerk.

"The bed and board was most excellent, my good man. Believe one who knows by experience."

"Thank you, Mist' Pembroke! Come again."

The man named Pembroke paid his bill from a fat roll of bank notes and carelessly shoved the remainder back in a pocket. As he stepped out the front door, a shiny buggy drawn by two fast grays pulled up at the sidewalk. The Spanish-looking man got out of it and helped Pembroke in with almost obsequious attention, arranging a carriage robe over his knees and holding a match to the cigar clenched between Pembroke's lips. Then, climbing to the driver's seat, the Spanish-looking man took up the reins and clucked to the grays. They moved off in a rush, the carriage disappearing on the east road from Monument.

Jessie watched all this, rubbing her chin thoughtfully. Then, with a pearly smile, she walked over to the desk clerk and remarked in a throaty voice, "My, that must be a very important person who just left."

"Oh, yes'm. That's Tobias Pembroke."

"What's he do?"

"Do? Why, eh, he stays here, he does."

Managing to keep her smile, she asked, "All the time?"

"No. This's his fourth visit."

The register lay open. Jessie read the names. Her own signature was there and so was Ki's, from when they had rented rooms the previous day. The last guest had been the elegant Tobias Pembroke, whose hometown, according to his writing in the registar, was Houston, Texas. What interested Jessie as much if not more was that his handwriting was round and even, each letter scrupulously formed, showing the determined character of the author and his intense application to details. She was certain that she had seen a

61

specimen of that writing before—on the death list in her pocket!

The discovery opened a mystifying and alarming vista to Jessie. Hacho Chown and his boss, Quaid Ruther, had loomed large, but from the facts she could now deduce that they were only agents, tools of a much cleverer, more dangerous man. Obviously Pembroke had written the list, and most likely he'd given it to Ruther, who in turn passed it to Hacho Chown. There had to be a mighty important reason for him to fashion such a death list, and to bring him four times to such a backwater burg as Monument—a motive for mass murder that must have also drawn him to tour the hill country, for undoubtedly Pembroke and his manservant were the ones Sam Oliphant had chanced upon a few months ago.

Of course, that still begged the question *Why?*

"If you don't mind my asking," Jessie said to the clerk, "who was the Spanish-looking chap with Mr. Pembroke?"

"That's Luis Gutierrez, his secretary and aide."

Suddenly Jessie whirled around, for a difference in the sounds from the noisy saloon warned her of danger. It was an abrupt menace, and she realized what it was as she saw Ruther's two gunmen confronting Ki. Ruther was still down the bar, a smirk on his face as he and everybody else in the saloon stared at the hardcases challenging Ki.

The pair was after blood and mayhem, nothing less.

★

Chapter 5

Although there had seemed to be no room at the
bar a few moments ago, there was plenty of space
cleared now, as men sought to get out of the line
of fire. Expert at judging the paths flying lead
might take, spectators silently set themselves. Ki
had turned with his back to the mirror and rail.
He had one heel hooked in the footrest and his
elbows on the edge of the bar. A wide-bodied man
in a black shirt and scratched riding leather, and
with a dark Stetson curved over his low brow, was
cursing Ki. Jessie could see the deep red of his
bull neck and glimpse a dirty cheek with beard
stubble on it.

"You stepped on my foot, you!" the hardcase
snarled. "Ain't there enough room in the world
without a slinky-eyed Chink havin' to walk all
over yore betters?"

Listening stone-faced to the violent abuse, Ki
reckoned he was facing a fight, likely a gunfight
before it was all over. It was a setup; he wasn't
going to be able to get out of it. As well-versed in
unarmed combat as he was, he could easily have
killed the hardcase, killed him and his buddy and

Ruther with lightning speed. But he intuitively perceived that using methods that would seem strange and exotic would draw too much attention and might later backfire against him and Jessie and, perhaps, against other Orientals, such as Fong Lu. He'd have to beat this hardcase at his own game, the cruder yet accepted technique of the common brawl.

And the best defense was an offense.

So Ki was offensive. "Run along, sonny, or I'll wash out your mouth with the spittoon for using such language."

Ridicule was one thing that such gunslinger's ego could not break, and the titter from the listeners goaded Ruther's man to blind fury. With a hoarse shout, he threw a punch at Ki, but Ki weaved his head aside and struck back with a jolting right-left to the man's stomach and heart. The attack caught the man surprised and unguarded, but he moved in undaunted, hammering with abandon. Ki shifted and feinted, evading the blows, stabbing two lefts to the man's face so fast that one had scarcely hit before the other had landed.

Then a roundhouse knuckler cracked alongside Ki's cheek, momentarily stunning him. Before he could recover, the man got an arm around him and smashed him twice in the face with stiff, short-range punches. Ki butted him hard, breaking free, and launched another one-two combination. His left opened a gash over the man's eye; the right flattened his nose. The man staggered, spurting blood from his nostrils, and the customers yelled.

For a second, it appeared the man was going to draw his revolver. But Ki, wanting to avoid gunplay if possible, taunted him by jeering, "Tuckered out, sonny? Can't take it, eh?"

Bellowing, the man dove, grappling, to wrap Ki in another crushing hug. But this time Ki was prepared, catching the man's already broken nose against his rising right knee. Pushing the man away then, Ki hit him a half-dozen more times in both eyes. Like a blundering, blind bear, the man tried to slug back, but Ki went under the swings and pummeled him in the belly and face, driving him the length of the bar. Dazed and bleeding, the man sagged to his knees, bewildered by the unleashed fury of Ki's assault.

Ki hauled the man to his feet, while the crowd closed in around them, baying for the finishing blow. They weren't disappointed. Ki brought his right fist up from somewhere down around his feet. It hit the man's chin with the sound heard in a slaughterhouse, when a steer was brained with a maul. The man arched backward and slid five feet along the sawdust-covered planks, coming to rest when his head struck the brass spittoon. He didn't get up.

The man's buddy, snarling, whipped out his revolver, the weapon rising and cocking under his blunt thumb as he pointed at Ki for the kill.

Two pistols seemed to explode simultaneously. Jessie had drawn and fired just as this second man's gun went off. Ki stood at the bar, a throwing dagger in hand, as the gunslinging buddy dropped his arm and fell on his face, wriggling in the blood-wet sawdust. Swiveling around, then, Ki focused on Quaid Ruther, knowing the freighter was the dangerous one.

Ruther was whipping a hand inside his jacket. He had a pistol in a shoulder holster and was reaching for it. Pushing through to the fore of the crowd, two more henchmen were drawing weapons as well.

To draw fire from the crowd and get some sort of bulwark between himself and the enemy guns, Ki threw himself across the bar, swiping several glasses and bottles off the counter.

"Outside, Ki!" Jessie shouted, even as she hurried a shot at Ruther. But as she raised her thumb off her pistol hammer, one of Ruther's followers darted between her and the freighter, and caught the heavy slug in the shoulder.

Guns were snapping, splintering the backbar mirror as Ki dove over the counter. Ruther's point-blank aim was wrecked as his own man blundered against him, howling with pain and clutching his right arm. The other gunslinger was blocked and shoved aside by retreating customers. Behind the bar, Ki was comparatively safe for the moment, but was well aware that Ruther and his men would swiftly bottle him up at both ends—and bobbing up, he glimpsed them already moving, preparing to sweep the aisle and kill him. He tossed his dagger to slow them, the knife catching a man in the shoulder, making him wince and crumple.

Stooped over, Ki hastened along the bar aisle toward the end closest to the lobby exit, stepping over the bartenders who were huddled flat on the planks. He was two-thirds down the aisle when his heel caught in something and threw him hard on the wet walkway. It was an iron ring in a trap door. He was up quickly, another knife in hand. Close by him was a quivering, fat bartender, scrunched under the bar, where copper tubing came up from the cellar. Ki bobbed up again to see to Ruther and his crew, flung his knife, and ducked just as a bullet cut his hat crown and smacked into the mirror. Then he leapt for the end of the bar and across to the lobby.

Lead dogged him. But Jessie was covering his escape, and sent a flurry of shots into the barroom. Ruther was forced to retreat, his men diving behind tables, and other customers stampeding to evade the blazing gunfire. In the chaotic pandemonium, Ki was able to make the exit. Jessie sent a couple more at Ruther, and by the time the freighter and his gun crew had recovered, Ki had reached the lobby and was partly sheltered by the wall.

Ruther began hooting and whistling as Jessie's tearing lead forced his head down. There was a brief lull in the fire, and gray powder smoke drifted to the heated areas around the hanging gilt oil lamps.

Crouched at the edge of the archway, Ki heard answering howls to Ruther's calls. "Ruther must have more men close at hand," he called to Jessie.

"And they're coming fast!"

Together they turned and raced out through the hotel exit, only to see seven or eight of Ruther's men running up the street.

A stentorian challenge came from the plaza. A lone man came galloping toward the Palace. "Halt there! Cut it out!"

"That's the marshal," Ki guessed. "A lot of help he'll be!"

The lone constable was brave enough as he charged toward the center of the disturbance. Quaid Ruther had thrown open a side window and was calling his men by name as he urged them into the fray. Ruther was hard, and as far as physical prowess went he was a dangerous opponent.

Ki was limping.

"Is it bad?" Jessie asked.

"No, just a burn along my calf," Ki answered. "We better sashay. No use making a fight here. They outnumber us, and they'll shoot us in the back if they get the chance."

Ducking under the hitchrail, Jessie and Ki mounted their horses and turned along Main. Quaid Ruther plummeted from the dark slit between the Palace and the next building, having climbed out the side window.

"There they go!" Ruther yelled, still calling up his crowd in a brassy voice. "They downed Nifty! Kill 'em!"

The main gang had come up now, and they all began sending shots after Jessie and Ki. But they had only a few brief glimpses of the fleeing pair as they galloped out of town, drawing out of easy revolver range. Ruther's fighting dander was up,

though, and he was swearing and shouting at his
followers, who were scrambling to obey, hitting
the leather of their mustangs and setting out after
the two.

The moon was up. The town road quickly petered
out into the main dirt trail running along the
bank of the river, with the rising hills showing
black against the silver sky. Dust swirled from
the beating hoofs.

Ki glanced back over a hunched shoulder. "Here
they come!"

They had a few hundred yards' start. Quaid
Ruther and perhaps ten more riders were bunched
together and were silhouetted against the lighted
settlement as they flogged and spurred their horses
in pursuit. Since her discovery of Tobias Pembroke,
however, Jessie had lost much of her interest in
Quaid Ruther. Contempt entered into her account
of Ruther, contempt for him and his thuggish
henchman Hacho Chown—dim-witted killers who
showed their hands and were marked for the law
and for vengeance. Behind his guise as freighter,
Ruther was an outlaw and no doubt a proficient
gunfighter in a knock-down-drag-out fight. But he
had no finesse. Tobias Pembroke loomed large in
Jessie's imagination. Because of Ruther's stupidity, she had been set on Pembroke's trail. She would
never leave it now until either she or Pembroke was
done for.

The trail angled away from the river and up
the long grade of a hillock. From its crest, they
could glimpse bobbing figures behind, silhouetted
in the moonlight as they dogged their dust-plumed

trail. They could hear not-so-distant shouts and an occasional gunshot, and Ki cautioned, "They're gaining."

Raking their horses' flanks, the two plunged down the other side of the hillock. At the bottom, they veered off the trail and charged pell-mell through the dark masses of boulders and scrub, then along an arroyo toward the river. They had trouble controlling their mounts as they skidded down one bank of the arroyo and up the other. They wheeled their horses and crossed again, then a third and then a fourth time. The dirt and gravelly sand cratered around their tracks, filling and flattening their depressions so that all sense of direction was confused.

With Ki in the lead, they started back toward the trail on the same path they'd made getting to the arroyo. When they spied Ruther and his crew cresting the hillock, they slowed their mounts to a dustless walk and, under cover of the large rocks and brush, cautiously began moving back in the direction of Monument.

Ruther and his crew hit bottom and almost passed where they had left the trail before someone spotted their path. The pursuers reined in. So did Jessie and Ki, hiding, motionless, a short distance from them in a patch of ocotillo and twisted yucca, their hands over their streaming horses' mouths to stifle any whinnies. Ruther and crew milled, then roared off toward the arroyo.

Jessie and Ki immediately started circling around them again, angling back to their path and then to the trail, their own tracks becoming lost in the welter of the others, their horses and hunching torsos masked by the night and their billowing spumes of dust. They contined straight across the trail and pressed on toward the range of rolling hills. Presently the river flatland rose to become foothills, and they began skirting twisted ravines and following rocky plateaus. After a time, they reined in by a small rill that cut down through a craggy ledge, and they dismounted, stiff and exhausted.

Their trembling, heaving horses sunk their muzzles gratefully to the water and nearby scratch grass. Jessie and Ki also drank from the stream, though there was nothing they could do for food, except pull up their belts a notch. The moon, emerging from behind banked clouds, illuminated the flats below—where somewhere, they reflected, rode Ruther and his crew like a posse, an outlaw posse still rabid to capture them. And posses were known to chase men for as much as a hundred miles, dispatching them where they found them, as summarily as possible.

"We'll have to chance it," Jessie observed. She, Ki, and their horses were too fatigued to continue without a rest.

They lay down in a hollow and dozed.

They did not sleep for long.

In the gray chill of early false-dawn, they were up and riding westerly, across the range of box-like hills, stony ridges, and brushy draws. They kept out of sight as much as possible, continually wary for sight or sound of any riders closing in on them.

71

Around mid-morning, they dipped down out of the hills into a valley that was particularily rocky and dotted with stunted growth. On the far side rose another section of broken and chopped uplands. They struck across it, and the deeper they went, the more like a barren labyrinth it became. They would dip through one hardpan canyon and then up to crown a naked crag, only to encounter another canyon, with yet another crag looming beyond it. It made them feel oddly forlorn just to look at the brutal, bleak expanse stretching about them.

By noon, they were slack in their saddles, less cautious of pursuit, logy from thirst, hunger, and the now oppressive heat. They let their horses seek their own slow pace, while they followed the meandering course of still another of the seemingly endless series of canyons. Along one slope, a couple of hundred yards above them, erosion had etched a slender shelf; it ran more or less parallel with the floor of the canyon and, because of numerous rocky overhangs, was dappled with shadow.

Jessie and Ki climbed to the shelf and jogged along it, more in search of relief from the sun now, than shelter from a trailing gun crew. Imperceptibly at first and then more and more obviously, the slopes became steeper and the canyon narrower, until finally not only the shelf but the canyon itself petered out in a cul-de-sac of blank walls. They stopped there for a much-needed break, frustrated at the dead end and the wasted time it represented, before they started the long trek back.

They were still returning, were almost to the point where they'd come upon the shelf, when a bullet plucked at the sleeve of Ki's shirt, the sound of the shot hard on it. Startled, they scrunched in their saddles and lashed their horses, glancing wildly about for sign of the attacker. They didn't have to look hard or far for the source.

Down on the canyon floor were two men. One was a stranger to them, a man with long, unkempt hair and ratty backwoods clothing; he was rising from where he'd been stooping over tracks their horses had left. "A tracker," Jessie surmised aloud, pressed into service by the other man—who was Hacho Chown, crouching on his knees to steady the Winchester he was aiming for his next shot. Ruther and his mob were nowhere to be seen, evidently having gotten tired of chasing blind leads and disgustedly packed it in. But no doubt Ruther still burned with blood lust, siccing his top man, Chown, and a tracker after them.

Frantically they sent their horses, snorting and reproachful of the slope, zigzagging to spoil Chown's aim. Bullets whined through the air and spurted dust around them, and Ki realized that they'd be cut down before they could reach the rim.

"If I can stall them," he called to Jessie, "we might make it!" He swerved toward a clump of boulders on his left, and, dismounting at a trot, dove behind them. Instead of merely hiding, hoping for Chown and the tracker to follow and come within easy pickin' range, Ki put his back to the largest of the rocks and pushed.

The boulder teetered in its earthen socket. Jessie, catching on to what Ki was trying to do, joined him and together they shoved, and the boulder fell, caroming down the slope. Quickly they moved to the next one, heaving against it until it pulled loose and went toppling. Then they worked on a third, sending it rolling.

Chown and the tracker had remounted and were partially up the steep grade. One shocked glimpse and they wrenched their horses sidelong to avoid the onrushing boulders. The horses shied, skewing and fishtailing, and sprang bucking back down the slope. Jessie and Ki, already plowing uphill again, could hear, above the thundering rocks, the horses' shrill whinnies and their riders' futile commands. But just before the two could have reached the crest, the men below managed to regain control of their panic-stricken mounts and open fire again.

Jessie and Ki plunged over the rim, dropping behind another crop of boulders as a fusillade chipped and ricocheted off the rock around them. Immediately they began pushing the boulders free and sent them tumbling. Peering over her shoulder, Jessie saw the tracker firing from astride his horse, while Chown had one foot on the ground and the other lodged in his stirrup, in the process of either stepping in or out of his saddle. The new avalance boogered Chown's horse again. It jerked the reins out of his hands and started dragging Chown by his hooked boot across the canyon floor. The tracker dashed after him. Their loud swearing was imaginative and fulsome.

Remounting, Jessie and Ki headed swiftly across the spine of the slope and into the wild fastness of the hills. They knew Chown would soon be on the prod again; nothing like a little anger, revenge, and bruised skinning to foster dedication to your job. But they were determined not to make it easy for Chown. They avoided open ground and skylines, and clung instead to drywash beds, enveloping brush, and rock—lots of hard, untrackable rock. They rode for the better part of the afternoon, until the winding canyons grew shallow and the ridges more rounded, and at last they came to a wide, gently rolling flatland.

A cattle trail ran lengthwise across the flat, the wispy grass trampled and gouged by hundreds of cattle and horse hoofs. they urged their horses down onto the flat and joined the trail, following it southerly and then easterly as it wandered through a succession of interconnecting valleys and canyons. After three or so miles, the trail skirted a nester's abandoned homestead on their left.

"Let's take a breather," Jessie suggested.

There were two dilapidated structures—a shack set up facing the trail, and a barn at its rear—at right angles, forming a kind of broken-linked L. They sat back a short ways into a field whose earth had once been broken by a plow then left to the weeds. In the crotch of the L was a rock-walled well topped by a creaky wooden windlass, from which an old galvanized tin bucket hung by a saddle rope.

Jessie viewed the 'stead with a different eye. As they walked their mounts off-trail toward the buildings, she murmured, "What a great spot to get caught in a crossfire. Let's get our drink and go."

Ignoring his gelding as it nudged his back, begging for water, Ki dunked the bucket deep in the well and cranked it to the surface. Despite the obvious thirst of the horses, though, neither animal drank long or full; indeed, they pulled back a bit, as though reluctant to drink at all. Only when the horses were done did Ki lower the bucket and draw it up to wash the dust from his and Jessie's throats. They took little sips, swallowing slowly, for the water had a bitter taste like quinine and soda, along with an odd rotten-egg smell.

Frowning thoughtfully, Jessie walked across the yard and into the weed-grown field. She kicked at the plow-loosened topsoil, then stooped and picked up a handful of dirt. It was dull yellow, with brownish and sometimes blackish veins streaked through.

"Look here, Ki," she remarked. "This's certainly strange-looking loam under the the topsoil."

"Doesn't look like it could grow much very well," he observed, nodding. "If this is throughout these hills, that might explain why plant life is so meager and stunted."

"I wonder . . ." Jessie, still pondering, scooped up another handful and crumbled the dirt clods through her fingers. Then, wiping her hands clean, she rose and said, "Well, we can't stay here, and I don't wish to lead Chown back to the Bar-B-Bar if

I can avoid it. Let's head back to Monument. It'll probably be evening by the time we get there. If we can't find Fong Lu tonight, I want to be at his laundry first thing tomorrow morning."

★

Chapter 6

Their cautious, circuitous return to Monument took longer than Jessie and Ki had expected, and night had long fallen by the time they sighted the lights of the town. Unwilling to risk another encounter at the Palace Hotel, they set up a cold camp a short distance away, in the brushy recesses of a secluded gorge. After a brief but thorough check to make sure they were alone and fairly well screened, they bedded down fully dressed. Both preferred the discomfort of sleeping clad and armed whenever camping out in wild country, and this night it was downright mandatory . . .

A cloudless sunrise was beginning to blaze above the eastern horizon, staining the hills a bloody red, as Jessie and Ki broke camp and headed for Monument. The crimson dawn had evolved into a warm, golden morning when they arrived in town. The laundry shop appeared open, a handful of elderly Chinese lounging outside its front door, sunning and gossiping the way old folks do. They ceased their chatter as Jessie and Ki dismounted and approached, eyeing the pair with poorly veiled suspicion.

Jessie couldn't blame them. These were uncertain times for the Chinese, due largely to politicans claiming that the hard times were the result of cheap coolie labor. There was talk of shipping all of the Orientals back to China, and if Greg Nehalem was right about a number of Chinese vanishing, their property confiscated, it was small wonder they were suspicious.

Ki, too, felt uneasy. "This isn't right," he murmured to Jessie. "Something's afoot here. You think it might be a trap?"

"I don't see how," Jessie said with a shake of her head. "In any event, we're going in."

The interior of the laundry shop was dimly lighted, and for a moment they were nearly blind as they stepped out of the bright sun glare of the dusty street. They halted just inside the door, conscious of the sweetish odor of incense in the air. Now they could make out a bronze Chinese god on a teakwood pedestal. The pedestal stood at one end of a long counter, behind which were shelves stacked with paper and string-wrapped laundry parcels, and a curtained doorway that no doubt led to a rear workroom.

The curtain rippled; a Chinaman stepped through. Sinewy and angular, almond-eyed, pigtailed, and darker complected than Ki, he stood all of five-five in faded denims and a butternut twill shirt. "Welcome, Miss Starbuck," he said gravely, bowing slightly from the waist. "And you, Ki."

"How did you know our names?" Jessie asked, wondering at the almost perfect English spoken by this Oriental stranger.

"We have a mutual friend," he answered, an ironic smile on his face. "I am Fong Lu, son of Fong Wah." With a nod of his head, Fong Lu indicated that they were to follow him through the curtain, then disappeared.

Quickly trailing after him, Jessie and Ki were led across the rear workroom, past Chinese girls laboring at washtubs or with heavy irons heated at blazing stoves. Fong Lu opened a small door at the rear, ushering them into a small, dim room. The furnishings were simple—a charcoal stove, two chairs, and a table. An unlighted candle was stuck in the neck of a wine bottle, while windows were covered with heavy drapes. Another door, in the very back wall, was heavily barred.

Lighting the candle, Fong Lu shut the workroom door and gestured for them to take seats. Jessie did so reluctantly, frowning, unsure how to bring up the murder of Fong Lu's father. Yet it had to be done, for she felt in that way she could help clear Nehalem.

"You know about your father?" she asked gently, watching Fong Lu's face.

"My father went west, disguised as a poor traveler," Fong Lu answered. "He wanted to see our friend, Lieutenant Nehalem, for he is of the military."

"And Fong Wah believed Nehalem could get the Army after the men who're persecuting your people?" Jessie guessed, and knew her assumption was correct, for Fong Lu nodded.

"I did not know my father had gone until it was too late to stop him," Fong Lu continued. "Friends told me. In some manner a man who calls himself Quaid Ruther followed. This man murdered my father or ordered it done, and put the blame on Greg Nehalem."

Jessie saw the grief that sprang into those almond eyes. "If that's the case—and I personally suspect it is—Quaid Ruther will pay."

"Yes, he will," Fong Lu declared bitterly. "He will pay dearly. In Peking, before my father and I came to your country, missionaries taught me I should forgive my enemies, that a good life is the best revenge. That is Western nonsense. Revenge is the best revenge."

"The law may have a stake in this, too," Jessie reminded him. "But how come you know all about Ruther and his involvement in your father's death?"

For the first time, Fong Lu's almond eyes narrowed and he drew himself stiffly erect. "Miss Starbuck," he said after a moment, "I am going to ask you a question. Do you believe Army courts to be infallible?"

Wondering at this strange question, Jessie looked up at Fong Lu a long moment before replying. "If you're referring to Greg Nehalem," she replied carefully, "I don't believe he's guilty— I never did."

Still Fong Lu's features were immobile. "Miss Starbuck, would you condone escape from military justice?"

A sudden fear leapt through Jessie like flame. "Greg!" she cried. "Did he try to escape?"

"Yes."

"If he killed anyone making that break, they'll hang him."

"He killed no one, Miss Starbuck," Fong Lu said with an inscrutable smile. "I am glad you feel as you do." He walked to the rear door, lifted the bar out of its slot, and opened the door.

A dirty, red-eyed figure strode into the room. It was Lieutenant Greg Nehalem, who by now should have been arriving at Fort Brown to begin serving a life sentence for murder. Shaken by emotion, Nehalem stood in the center of the small room, then leapt forward to grasp Jessie's hand in his own, murmuring her name through stiffened lips as if in prayer.

Fong Lu barred the door again. "The lieutenant came to me last evening," he explained.

"What happened?" Jessie demanded. "Greg, did you—?"

"I tricked Wolcott," Nehalem said, sinking wearily into a chair. "It was easy to fool a man like him, who had his head crammed with West Point theory. It seems the textbooks didn't cover a situation like this. I made my break at night. The men did not try too hard to cut me down. I rather suspect they fired over my head." It was evident that he had been in mad flight since his break from the Army escort. Somewhere along the way, he had discarded his uniform; now he wore patched corduroy pants, a torn cotton shirt, and an old sweat-stained hat. He did not explain what had happened to his uniform, and Jessie did not ask, as he added, "I hardly ate or slept. My one thought was to get here, to Fong Lu and . . . and Adriane."

83

"The next step is to keep out of the Army's way," Jessie said thoughtfully. "Has Lieutenant Wolcott trailed you?"

"I don't know. I suppose he's picked up my trail by this time. He'd like nothing better than to see me hanged."

"You've got to be careful or he may get his chance."

A wild look swept into Nehalem's bloodshot eyes. "But I've got to see Adriane! I can't stand it that she doesn't know how things are."

Quickly Jessie told of meeting Adriane Bryce, the attack on the ranch, and the disappearance of her father. "The main thing you've got to do is stay out of sight," she advised.

"But—"

"Ki and I will go see Adriane for you," Jessie said firmly. "There's no telling where Wolcott will be looking for you, and Quaid Ruther and his crew are running loose around these parts as well. They'd shoot you on sight."

"They can try," Nehalem answered defiantly. "I'd gladly die to gun Ruther down for killing Fong Wah."

As he said the last, a shadow of sorrow crossed Fong Lu's eyes at the mention of his father's death. But instantly it was gone. "No, my good friend Greg, Ruther is not worth your death. Miss Starbuck is right. You should stay under cover here, at least temporarily."

Leaving Greg Nehalem sitting slumped and morose, Fong Lu ushered Jessie and Ki back through the shop to the street. No soldiers were in sight, or tough hombres who might have been Ruther gunmen.

Mounting, Jessie thanked Fong Lu. "Assure Greg that we're riding straight to the Bar-B-Bar to talk to Adriane," she said. Then, as they started heading out of town, she explained to Ki: "I'd have preferred to head for Houston and locate this Tobias Pembroke. But we've got to tell Adriane of Greg's escape. She's got a level head. She'll send a note back to Greg, telling him that it isn't wise for them to meet now. Otherwise . . ." She drew a finger like a knife blade across her throat.

The sun was high in the morning now, and the world was lovely. Nearby ran the river, and the round hills rose above it like a series of rolling knuckles. The valley road, which had been such a danger spot the last couple of nights, was empty and stretched along in a winding ribbon. In the blue sky here and there could be seen stains of smoke where some farm or other settler's home stood.

Presently they reached the lane that led from the wagon road to the Bryce ranch house. The lane was shadowed by tall brush and a canopy of trees, and it was fortunate that these shielded Jessie and Ki from the house, for just as they were about to enter the yard, they heard voices— the loud voices of the foreman Moss and of an authoritarian, even arrogant, stranger.

Quietly dismounting, they led their horses off the lane and tethered them in the covering brush, then padded around to where they could see and hear what was going on. Ki whistled silently in surprise as he followed Jessie's pointed finger and saw the blue-clad soldiers grouped on the ranch-house porch.

Confronting Moss was an Army officer—an officer they recognized as Lieutenant Dunton Wolcott. The hot Texas sun had burned young Wolcott's face so that the skin was peeling in several places, which did not add to his West Point dignity. His uniform showed good tailoring and gave him a well-cut figure, but at the moment it was not so natty. It was dusty, and even from this distance, Jessie and Ki could see that he was thoroughly angry.

"I'm plumb sorry," Moss said, his voice carrying to them. "Miss Bryce ain't here. She left this dawn for White Mule."

"Was anybody with her?" Wolcott demanded, and gave a brief description of Greg Nehalem.

"Naw, she rode off alone," Moss answered. "Her pa's been missin', and she went up thataway to look for him."

Jessie and Ki watched the lieutenant and his five troopers walk around the corner where their horses were tied, mount, and ride off. Then, recovering their own horses, they rode on into the yard, pulling up by the porch where Moss still stood, hands on hips, scowling in the direction of the departed squad. Upon seeing them, his glare turned to a grin.

"Light down a spell," he said, greeting them. "You just missed the action."

"No, we didn't," Jessie replied as they joined Moss on the porch. Explaining how they had over-heard his exchange with Lieutenant Wolcott, she concluded by asking the old foreman, "What do you think of Adriane going after her father?"

"I wish she hadn't done so," Moss answered grimly. "That part of the country ain't no place for a woman like her. Frankly, what needs to be done most at present is get a shipping herd together. The ranch has a note to meet the first of the month."

"Who holds the note?" Jessie asked.

"Fayette County Bank an' Trust. Mist' Bryce did a prime job of stocking last year an' the year afore, figurin' he had to have a better breed of stock if it was goin' to compete with others in the open market. Reckon he was right, but he had to put the outfit into debt to do it. And of course he didn't expect the trouble that's come to us since. Now, with him gone, things are worsenin'. Almost all my riders are gettin' on in years, and with Chuck wounded an' all, we're shorthanded to boot. I wisht the Ol' Man was here, or even his daughter, who has the smarts like her pa to make decisions and direct operations the way they orter."

Jessie nodded, understanding more than Moss thought. Clearly the foreman was a cow-savvy puncher who had the loyalty of his crew and the confidence of the Bryces. But as was the case on many small spreads, he as foreman served more as an assistant to his boss, and little as an independent leader on his own. This was not only his position, but his *dis*position, his second nature after so many years, and now he felt adrift. And Jessie felt torn. On the one hand, she very much wanted to get to Houston and discover just who and what Tobias Pembroke was. On the other, she couldn't leave the Bar-B-Bar to go bust, not if there was something that might quickly and readily turn matters around.

After a thoughtful moment, she said, "Moss, Ki has taken charge of a lot of gathers on the Circle Star and other ranches. I can't speak for him, on whether he'd be willing; but if you'd be willing and your crew would go along, he'd make a very fine *segundo* for the next couple of days or so."

"Be willing? Why, I'd be plumb honored, and I reckon the crew would be, too! The Starbuck handle has a top-notch reputation." Moss turned to Ki. "What'cha say? Will you help us out?"

Ki, somewhat taken aback by Jessie's suggestion, considered a moment. "Okay, Moss, I'll take a stab at it. I never yet saw a spread where a resolute crew couldn't chouse a hefty passel of fat beefs from the brakes and canyons. I'd bet we'll find that's the condition on the Bar-B-Bar. Once we're done gathering, where do you figure on driving the herd?"

"There's a buyer in Houston Ol' Man Bryce always dealt with."

Ki glanced at Jessie. "Well, this's one way of getting to Houston, I suppose." Then, to Moss: "Now tell me a little about the spread and the things that need to be done."

"If'n you like to, we'll ride over it now, together," Moss said. "But I got a notion things will change from now on."

Jessie smiled. "Yes, I've a notion they will . . ."

Before that day's ride was over, Ki had decided that the Bar-B-Bar was a good spread but a hard one to work. A goodly portion of it was heavily grown with dagger, prickly pear, and other similar chaparral. The whole west range, which shouldered against the hills, was a labyrinth of gorges and canyons.

"Fine place for cows to hole up in bad weather," he commented to Jessie and Moss, "but an almighty tough chore to get them out."

Some time later, from where they sat their horses on the crest of a rise, they could gaze across a large expanse of hill country. The stretch before them was devoid of growth save for a sparse straggle of *sacaguista* grass.

"This's the utterly worthless portion of the ranch," Moss told them. "Ain't it strange that nothin' will grow here 'cept that salt grass? There's not a bush or a tree to be found anywhere."

On the following day, the Bar-B-Bar outfit got busy assembling a shipping herd to replace the one stolen the night of Jessie and Ki's arrival at the ranch. As Moss had told them, all of the riders were men advanced in years. Ki found that they were efficient, within their physical limitations, thoroughly conversant with the various ramifications of the cow business, but slow in their work, and decidedly old-fashioned in their notions. And the spread was, as he had suspected, a hard one to work. The cows were difficult to fog out of their hole-ups in the brush and in the canyons. Moss declared they had "come right out of the Gulf of Mexico. That's what makes 'em so damned salty!"

They were fat and sleek, however, in prime condition, and with plenty of meat on their bones—the kind of beefs buyers were glad to get.

Several busy days followed. A shipping herd was steadily collected, its growing numbers bunched in a box canyon with a narrow mouth and sheer rock sides. The floor of the canyon supported a rich bed of grass, fed by a small stream that foamed from a crack in the end wall and wound through to flow out the mouth.

When Moss had first shown Ki and Jessie the canyon, he had bragged, "Ain't it a beaut? Ol' Man Bryce always holds his herds here in this hole instead of out in the open somewheres. It's a plumb natural corral. Nobody could come at 'em except from the front, and they'd have to ride around in back of 'em before they could start 'em, and I reckon me and the boys would have somethin' to say about that."

"Suppose somebody was holed up in there?" Ki had suggested.

"Huh, nobody could get in there," Moss scoffed. "The canyon is a box, and the sides and end wall are straight up and down. A lizard would get dizzy tryin' to come down them rocks. Anyway, anybody that wanted to get in would have to pass the boys. Nope, there's nothin' to worry about on that score . . ."

Now, days later, with the shipping herd ready to take the trail the next morning, Ki stood conversing with Jessie and Moss on the bank of the stream. He turned to study the site of the trail herders' camp, which was on a grassy flat in the canyon mouth. He glanced up at the dark gorges. Then, suddenly his attention became fixed on the surface of the little stream that purled at their feet. After a moment's silence, he turned to the ranch foreman.

"Moss," he said, "I'm thinking that's a mighty poor place to make camp. Suppose something happened to set the cattle off. They'd hightail right in this direction, and the camp would be right in their path."

"I put it here to keep 'em from strayin' out of the canyon," Moss explained. "They won't come past the fire. Nothin' to worry about on a night like this. Plumb still and quiet. If it was stormy, it would be somethin' else again."

"Just the same," Ki insisted, "you'd better move your trail crew's camp up onto that ledge under the cliff."

"You're loco—" Moss began, then glanced at Jessie.

"If Ki says you should move it," she told him, "I figure you'd better move it."

Moss shook his head in a bewildered fashion. "You got any particular reason for reckonin' it ought to be moved?"

"Yes," Ki said laconically, "I have."

Moss started to speak, apparently thought better of it, and grumbled instead. "Okay, we'll move it, but I bet afore mornin' y'all will wish you was sleepin' down here on this soft grass instead of up in them hard rocks. I can stand it if y'all can. I got more cushionin' on my bones than you have on yours."

The Bar-B-Bar punchers also grumbled, but there were evidently not in the habit of disobeying orders. "What about the fire?" one of them asked. "Shall we put it out?"

"Leave it alone," Ki said, and he added emphatically, "It'll be quite a spell before it burns down."

Grumbling a little more, the men drank their coffee beside the fire, then scrambled up through the deepening darkness to the rocky bench under the cliff. The horses were rope-corralled beside a thicket just to the right of the canyon mouth. The crew and Moss spread their blankets on the softer spots of the rock and were soon fast asleep.

Jessie and Ki also spread their blankets and lay down, but not to sleep. Half-reclining against a convenient boulder, Jessie gazed over the rangeland to the south of the canyon, thinking deeply, and decidedly awake. A short distance away, Ki settled on the west side of the canyon mouth; across from him was the waning fire, then the meandering bed of the stream.

Several hours passed. The moon wheeled westward, the stars burned golden, their luster dimmed by a film of clouds. The night was very still, with only the occasional contented rumbling of the cattle to break the silence . . .

More hours passed . . .

Jessie was still looking toward the ranch when she first thought she detected movement. Yet it was too distant and too dark for her to glimpse any detail. Then the movement was gone, leaving her with only an unpleasant premonition.

All remained calm . . .

For almost another hour she lay quiet. Then, abruptly, a sound came through the stillness, a *snap* that brought her bolt upright on her blanket. It was such a sound as was made by a boot breaking a dry branch, and it seemed to come from the blackness near the canyon mouth. Although Ki didn't wear boots, she couldn't help wondering at first if the noises were him moving about. Then came a soft, breathless whisper:

"Jessie!"

She sat listening intently, every nerve strung tight. She heard the faint crackling of underbrush off to her left.

"Jessie! It's me, Greg!"

She gasped, recognizing the voice. "Over here!"

The crackling of brush grew louder, closer. Nehalem stumbled into view, panting for breath, still garbed in old civilian clothing, now looking more tattered than ever. "Jessie, they're right behind—"

"What? Who?"

"Ran into 'em, whole bunch of 'em . . . Kilt my horse—"

With paralyzing suddenness, then, pandemonium broke loose in the black canyon. There was a roar of gunfire, a wild yelling, the snap and crackle of swung slickers, a drumroll of beating hoofs. Jessie bounded to her feet, hearing the cattle milling wildly and bellowing with fright. As the bewildering uproar behind them continued, they fled madly down the canyon, their hooves clashing on the stones, their terrified bawls adding to the turmoil.

★

Chapter 7

Tense and alert at the mouth of the canyon, Ki
watched the herd thunder past. Close on the heels
of the panic-stricken cattle came shadowy horsemen, yelling and shooting. Up behind him in the
rocks, Moss and his punchers were out of their
blankets, roaring profanity. Although dazed and
half-awake, they instinctively sized up the situation, grabbed their rifles, and began shooting.

The exultant yells of the rustlers changed to
howls of surprise and alarm. There was a scream of
pain that ended in a choking rattle. A man pitched
headlong from his saddle. In the next breath another fell like a sack of old clothes. Abruptly leaving
the cattle to scatter, the rustlers, low in their saddles, began charging toward the boulders where
the ranch hands were holed up. A third outlaw
somersaulted backward; two more vaulted their
horses over his sprawling body, only to be downed
in turn. The others kept coming, spreading up into
the rocks. All of a sudden, Moss and the punchers
were in a desperate bind, Ki realized. They had surprised the rustlers and accounted for a handful of
casualties without receiving a wound. But instead

of fleeing, the rustlers were counterattacking, in numbers that would overwhelm the defenders in short order.

"To the horses!" Moss roared. "Git to the horses!"

The punchers fell back, hustling through the rocks to where their horses were corralled. The rustlers were swarming up through the rocks and trees, turning both sides of the canyon mouth into an inferno of blazing gunfire.

Darting along between the boulders, Jessie and Nehalem pushed through to the horses. Ki, spotting them, angled off to intercept them, firing his carbine as he went, in an effort to cover their retreat. Jessie had a foot poised in one stirrup when Ki closed to grab his fractious gelding.

"Ki!" Nehalem yelled. "Look out!"

Jessie, too, caught the wink of steel as a rustler burst up through the brush for a point-blank shot at Ki. Hastily she drew her revolver and fired, but her bullet only creased the man's shoulder, failing to stop him. Frantically Nehalem hopped up and threw a large rock, which beaned the man smack in the middle of the forehead. Cussing in shock and pain, he reeled back out of his saddle and landed hard on his rump. That gave Ki the moment he needed; he sprang, using a forward snap-kick followed by a sideways elbow smash to cave in the rustler's ribs and stop his heart.

"Ride!" Nehalem urged impatiently. "Ride!"

Jessie mounted. Ki had a momentary delay while he fought his spooked, rearing horse, but finally he hurled himself into the saddle and jabbed both heels into the horse's flanks. The moro tore off in a lather. Jessie slewed her grulla mare about, ignoring the bullets coming ever closer.

"My hand!" she called to Nehalem. "Grab my hand!"

Nehalem caught Jessie's outstretched hand, seemingly without looking, and whipped up and around behind her.

Jessie shifted in the saddle, roweling her spurs. "Hang on!"

"I never fall," Nehalem retorted, then almost did. Slipping, rocking, he snatched the butt of Jessie's carbine, which was poking up from her saddle scabbard. The carbine came out in his hand, and wobbling precariously, he groped furiously with his free left hand for some steadying buttress and, not surprisingly, latched onto Jessie. Onto her left breast, to be exact.

Startled, Jessie sat straight up, momentarily speechless. Nehalem was not kneading or mauling; he was simply cupping her breast as if unaware or unconcerned about what he was using for support. Jessie was very aware. Her shock quickly waned, and she was about to protest when Nehalem finished settling and dropped his hand. So she dropped her fuss, not very concerned, really. Not in comparison to how she felt about the rustlers surging in around them, firing more wildly than ever.

Down toward the flat rangeland they galloped, smack-dab into the broken line of outlaws charging uphill. They had to brave it, though. So did Ki, Moss, and the punchers, who were bending over their horses' withers, their mounts chewing up the

97

ground as they scattered from the rampaging rustlers, their weapons blazing to cut off pursuit. The crescendoing battle rang over the terrain, pistols bucking, lead searching, horses galloping, their riders bracing against the expected punch of lead through their flesh, while the Bar-B-Bar shipping herd flowed out of sight under a cloud of dust that glinted silver in the moonlight.

Jessie hit the base of the slope, her horse almost floundering as it fought for a hold on the gravelly earth. Ki was nowhere in sight now, but rustlers were. Nehalem tisted around and triggered the carbine. Three stabs of flame leapt from its muzzle, three sharp reports blending as one—and three stupefied men fell, writhing, from their saddles.

How Nehalem chambered so quickly, or kept his perch against the recoil, was a mystery to Jessie. But then, Nehalem and the mess he was in was all a big mystery to her, making the man all the more intriguing to her, piquing her interest and personal attraction, and . . . to be honest, an awareness budded from his hand on her breast that bordered on sexual arousal. Not that she had any such designs in mind, she thought hastily; her only desires were to get out of this gun battle alive. At the moment, escape was her passion.

When Nehalem suddenly emptied three saddles, it took a lot of steam out of the rustlers who were chasing them, that particular bunch slowing, pulling rein. Nobody was eager to be in front. They were still pursuing, though, still winging salvos of lead, and Jessie knew that if they stuck true to form, they'd soon pick up the pace and return to their old blood-lust frenzy.

Deciding to take advantage of the opportunity while she could, Jessie pushed her tuckering mare into a mad gallop to increase the distance. It was a bone-jarring ride. The horse moved with all the smooth glide and coordination of a threshing machine. Nehalem scrunched in tighter behind her, clasping her firmly around the waist with one arm. They outran sight of the rustlers who'd taken after them; for that matter, they outran sight of all the other rustlers and all the Bar-B-Bar crew, and the mare was showing the effects, blowing like a penny-whistle. Nehalem leaned forward and said into Jessie's tender coral-pink ear: "Are you Apache? Do you eat the raw guts once you've killed her?"

Jessie gave a laugh and checked the horse to a trot. "I don't run horses to death, Greg—"

A bullet whined by, very close, making Nehalem flinch. Glancing behind, they glimpsed the dark moving bulge of tightly knit riders heading their way. Jessie raked her spurs, and the weary grulla bolted forward as a torrent of bullets pursued them. Nehalem swiveled around and sighted the carbine, but, muttering about long range and few cartridges, he then turned frontward and hugged Jessie around her waist. They both were acutely aware that the mare was exhausted, and the handful of rustlers behind them was gaining.

"Well, at least they'll be coming into range," Nehalem remarked philosophically.

Now slugs began snapping around them, plowing the dirt at their feet and spanging off the surrounding rocks. As they rode past a place where the wall of a bank had crumbled, Nehalem directed Jessie that way, and she sent the mare scrambling up the pile of loose rock and into the flanking undergrowth. The rustlers riddled the brush with gunfire. The darkness was alive with the snap and whine of bullets. Rugged rocks and spurs loomed close, allowing cover, and again Nehalem drew Jessie's attention, this time to the dark mouth of a narrow culvert. Its stone walls loomed high enough to offer shelter that the bouldered rises and flat rangeland could not, although Jessie was leery that this miniature canyon might turn out to be a box that would trap them.

She bent low over her horse's withers, hoping the flagging animal would not give out under them. Suddenly she stiffened. "Greg? Greg, what're you doing?"

What he was doing was cupping her breast again. This was no damned "error" like the first time! In one fell swoop he had his hand slid up the front of her shirt, and she could feel his thumb and forefinger rolling her nipple, tweaking it into hardness.

"Stop it, Greg! Greg?"

If Nehalem had anything to say for himself, he had no chance to tell it, as the pursuing rustlers sent a raging salvo their way. Jessie sensed a slight tremor of response to Nehalem's caresses, but choked it down, concentrating instead on eluding the riders who were trying to cut them off before they could reach the refuge of the rocks. Stuttering volleys of lead chased after them as they plunged into the culvert. It made a turn, then another, and the slopes grew steeper. They saw a slim secondary gully off to one side and veered into its narrow mouth, then twisted up into the rocks. Knowing it would be rank folly to try hiding at this point, they continued climbing the steep grade, setting off a minor avalanche of loose shale and gravel.

Just before they cleared the crest, they glimpsed the small band of rustlers reaching the base of the long slope. The men, still adamantly on their tail, started up but were forced to wrench aside to avoid the tumbling rock slide. The horses skewed and fishtailed, bucking back down. The rustlers swore luridly. Jessie's mare pawed its way to the top of the rim and, panting, paused for a moment to catch its breath.

"Ride!" Nehalem urged. "Here isn't safe!"

Jessie prodded the horse to get moving. "I'm not sure anywhere is safe with you."

"True, true," he murmured, his lips brushing her ear. "It's all this excitement. Makes you exciting, makes me excited."

"All it makes me is scared," she countered. "Scared and dirty and very tired." Yet she could feel perversely erotic throbs tingling up through her flesh as he continued stroking her gently, gently . . . until, despite herself, she moaned softly, having little inclination and absolutely no time to resist his fingers while they rode on into the wild fastness of the hills. She knew the rustlers would catch up again, and was determined not to make it sooner than need be by diverting her attention to Nehalem, but to keep focused on avoiding open ground and skylines, clinging instead to rock and brush. Especially brush. And shortly, as they wound along the jagged slopes, the brush grew heavy with briars and thorny weeds.

The sound of crashing horses came through to them from their right, toward the flats. They dove into the briar thickets as the horses trampled nearer, the riders peppering shadows with enraged abandon. Jessie pleaded and cajoled and pummeled her mare on through the stinging thorns and nettles. Behind them was total chaos—shouts, the whinnying of balky horses, the uneven rattle of gunfire. Thwarted from entering the briars, the rustlers tore off around to hit their quarry coming out, but they were too late. Chased by scattered shot, Jessie and Nehalem were blurs drumming into yonder roughlands. The shots did not cease until they were long out of sight and range.

After another quarter mile, Jessie slowed and let the exhausted mare seek its own pace. Heart pounding, she listened to the rustlers fade in the wrong direction, feeling less worried now about pursuit, and stirred by Nehalem to a feverish arousal. His fingers were kneading one sensitive breast, then the other, teasing her hardening nipples. His gentle kissing of her earlobe and the nape of her neck combined with the ministrations of his fingers to evoke in her an erotic stupor. She found herself watery and trembly when, forging through an acreage of brush and briar, they came upon a small clearing where the dirt was too hard to

102

sustain even the meagerest of thistles.

"I think we lost 'em," Nehalem said. "For a while."

"You bastard," she moaned, slumping from the saddle. "You got me gasping like a spavined mule."

Nehalem chuckled, then sagged to the ground, gritting his teeth as blood swelled from his thigh.

"You're wounded!"

"Just a crease," he growled, gripping his thigh.

Jessie bent quickly. "We'll have to get you to a doctor. All I can do now is clean the wound and stop the bleeding." To get to the thigh wound, she had to open his pants. Her hands dealt surely with the buttons of his fly, and he raised his hips to allow her to slide them down. Then he sank flat with a low, short grunt. Jessie, staring with something akin to trepidation, wondered if his grunt was of pain from his wound, or of relief from her releasing his big, stiff, crotch-trapped erection.

The wound proved to be quite minor, a clean furrow of the sort that bled profusely without much injury. Taking her first aid kit from her saddlebags, she wadded and bound his wound with gauze bandage, determined to ignore his jutting manhood, but finding it as hard for her as it was hard for him . . . and worse, just as she was done, she accidently brushed his meaty shaft.

Groaning, he tugged her to him, pressing his lips tightly against hers. The kiss was long. Ending it gradually, he held her tight before letting her go.

Trembling, Jessie said, "I don't know why I let you do that."

"You wanted it," Nehalem said, grinning. "And you know it."

"That's not so," she protested, eyes fever-bright. "I'm not excited. I told you, I'm scared, tired, and dirty."

"You can't sleep or wash now, and your fear is natural. It sharpens yours senses," he murmured in a husky voice that sent chills along her spine. "We're alert, aware, alone for this one short time. Why not do as we feel? As I've felt ever since we were children playing together?"

"That's just it, Greg, we were children."

"Not anymore. We've grown up."

"Well, you certainly have." Something prompted Jessie to gaze fully at him—something she sensed rather than reasoned; something in his presence, in his eyes as they took their slow, bold fill of her, in his touch as he drew her down to him again. And as their lips melted together once more, she knew she was no longer tired. Why not? She wanted him and they were staying awhile. She was caught up in an electric frenzy that seared a fiery path along her nerves. They kissed again, and again, lingeringly . . .

Almost before she was fully aware of it, Nehalem was undressing her. Jessie felt mesmerized. She would have been unable to fight his dexterous fingers even if she'd wanted to, as he peeled her shirt off and fondled her naked breasts. Garment by garment, they stripped nude. Then they stretched out on their impromptu bed of clothing. Jessie stroked between his thighs, Nehalem caressing her soft, flaxen curls and tender nether lips.

Buttocks tightening, Jessie arched her pelvis against his prowling fingers. Her liquid eyes closed and a gentle sigh escaped from her mouth as he rubbed her sensitive cleft, sliding a finger inside her. He slipped a second finger in, and she gasped with pleasure, her body undulating in response to his hand while he massaged her flesh to yearning arousal.

"I . . . I'm ready," she mewed. "But, but your wound . . ."

"Climb on."

Jessie rose, squatting, and straddled his hips, feeling his hot length burning against her crotch. She reached under with her right hand and grasped him, positioning his thick crown between her moist crevice, her loins absorbing his stabbing shaft as she lowered herself slowly yet eagerly upon it. Her stiffened nipples and aching breasts flattened against his muscular chest while she impaled herself completely, until the last inch of him was driven, throbbing, deep up inside her belly.

He asked, "Too much? Hurt?"

"Yes . . . *no!*" Jessie wriggled on him and felt his swollen girth flexing within her. She began sliding on him, slowly at first, then with increasing enthusiasm as the sensations intensified. Soon she was rearing high until his erection was almost totally exposed, then plunging down to ensheathe him fully, gasping, trembling, as his shaft surged into her depths like a fleshy bludgeon.

Nehalem shifted one hand to massage her jiggling breasts, toying harshly with her nipples.

In turn, she lowered her head and their mouths fused together, their tongues touching and flicking in play. Her pounding thighs matched his pumping upthrusts, her moist channel squeezing, squeezing, while he pummeled her with spiraling delight.

"Oh! Oh!" she chanted, enraptured.

He was spearing higher and faster into her moist passage. She shivered and moaned, quickening tempestuously, sensing her orgasm gathering tensely. Then Jessie felt his thrusting manhood swell, saw his eyes sparkle with a lusting urgency that drove him on. He was gasping hoarsely with imminent climax when Jessie cried out her own delirious peak, her fingers clawing his chest with wanton ecstasy.

"Ahhh . . . !"

Like a bucking bronco, she arched and plunged, feeling Nehalem vibrant and huge as he geysered up into her depths. His hands were on her buttocks, squeezing and relaxing, squeezing and relaxing, as though to help milk his pulsating eruptions . . .

Finally, with a sigh of satiation, Jessie slithered forward, releasing his deflating erection. He wrapped his arms around her in an affectionate hug, and she pressed tighter, stifling a contented yawn. "Just for a few minutes," she murmured. "Then we'll get dressed . . ."

For a while they just lay quietly, nuzzling and trading lazy kisses. Jessie hadn't lied to him; she'd been tired. Despite that, he'd managed to stoke her fires to a blazing pitch, to an inferno that had consumed them both. But now, in the aftermath, the fires were banked, and she nestled lethargically in his embrace. Yet Nehalem grew strangely restless . . . and then she felt his flaccid girth regaining hardness and length.

"Oh, my God," she moaned, quivering. She was drained, enervated, yet as Nehalem began a gentle thrusting against her, she found that her loins were responding in kind. "You'll rut me to death. Will you eat my raw guts then?"

"Not exactly what I'd in mind."

She began undulating responsively, her clitoris tingling with each pushing impact against his reviving shaft. He kissed her lips, her cheeks, and the tender hollow of her neck. Then he slipped lower, darting his tongue across her nipples, moving it wetly along her abdomen, rekindling passions within her belly. Then still lower, his lips probing and exploring as she whimpered, her fingers tangling in his hair while he worked down and thrust deep into her inner flesh. Her thighs clenched spasmodically around his laving tongue and nibbling lips, tendrils of arousal rippling up from her loins.

Nehalem pressed closer and reached up with both hands to play with her breasts, his mouth becoming a hot, hungry invader, licking with his tongue, nipping with his lips and teeth. She began to pant explosively, her groin grinding against his face with pulsing tension—a tremoring like the advance of a sundering earthquake. Again she poised breathless, tensing, straining—

Nehalem broke free and rose on an elbow. "Someone's coming."

107

"Me, dammit!"

In a scrambling leap, Nehalem grabbed the carbine. Jessie stared, trembling and frustrating, snapping as he vaulted toward the fringe of the clearing. "Why, that wound doesn't hurt you at all!"

"I told you it was just a crease." He hunkered, listening. "Riders approaching, I hear the horses."

"Lying won't help you! You knew it was a scratch, and you tricked me into dropping your trousers—" Jessie stopped, able to catch the sounds of saddle gear and movement through underbrush. The sensual spell shattered, she bolted up. "Who are they? Rustlers?"

"Nope! Ki and Moss!"

Frantically they sprang for their clothes.

"Where're my pants?" Jessie cried. "Of all the fool times!"

Nehalem had to laugh. "Be thankful. A couple of minutes earlier or later, and we'd never have noticed them!"

They heard Ki call out, "Don't shoot!" to avoid a mistake.

The underbrush parted, and into the clearing walked Ki, leading his horse, followed by the foreman Moss astride his cow pony. A moment was spent acknowledging one another, with surprise and relief and a few explanations tossed in.

"We got blocked at the canyon," Moss said. "After we shook our pursuit, we spotted owlhoots out an' about huntin', so we decided we'd better find what'd become of you folks, and hope we weren't too late."

"You could *never* have been *too* late," Nehalem replied deadpan, evading a shin kick from Jessie as he returned to the edge of the clearing. While stuffing an errant shirttail into his pants, he studied their backtrail and remarked, "I'm more worried we were too easy to find. How'd you know where we were?"

"Ki did. Don't ask me how," Moss answered. "Any more'n how he figgered them wideloopers might be lurkin' up in that canyon. He must be part bloodhound, I swear."

"I'm nothing of the kind," Ki retorted, disliking such flattery. Tracking to him was just common sense, and close attention to details and habits, but he added somewhat facetiously, "Finding this hiding place was simple. Since the rustlers hadn't caught you, you couldn't be where they were, so I simply looked where they weren't." It was then Ki noticed Nehalem stuffing in the shirttail and, glancing back at Jessie, saw that she didn't have her left boot on snugly. And he reckoned maybe he shouldn't ask a natural question like "What've you been doing?" So instead he hastened on with explaining about how he'd caught on to the rustlers hiding up in the canyon:

"Remember back when we were standing on the stream bank," he said. "Well, I was looking down into the stream, and I saw something come floating along on top of the water. It was a cigarette butt. None of your punchers were on the stream bank higher up at the time, Moss, so I figured that butt must have come down the stream out of the canyon. It couldn't have come far, either.

Otherwise the paper would've soaked off and it would've sunk. I figured the only way it could've got into the water was by some careless gent up there a little ways flipping it into the stream after he'd finished his smoke. Right then was when I decided the flat was no place for a camp."

Moss shook his head in admiration. "Them eyes of yores don't miss a thing, do they! I reckon we owe you plenty, Ki. If it hadn't been for you tanglin' their twine, right now me'n the boys wouldn't be anything much but grease spots. Wal, supposin' we start headin' back and get the boys t'gether. I've a notion there won't be much sleepin' tonight, roundin' up that scattered herd of ours."

"Another day," Jessie consoled him, "and you'll have that herd ready to roll."

"I certainly hope so," Moss told her anxiously. "The money them cows will bring will just about cover the payment due on that note the bank holds. I hate to think what'll happen if we fail to make that payment, or what I'd hafta tell Miz Adriane when she gets back."

"You'll make it," Jessie assured the foreman. "This time next week, your herd will be rolling east from Houston."

"When Adriane gets back?" Nehalem demanded, looking startled. "Whaddyuh mean, get back? Where is she?"

"Why, she's gone to White Mule to look for Mist' Bryce," Moss answered.

"Then she doesn't know I'm free!" Nehalem's teeth were clenched so hard that his jaw muscles ribbed out on either side, and there was a wild look in his eyes. "There's a lot of rustlers downed around here. I reckon I can pick up a revolver and a horse, and can head out for White Mule pronto!"

"Won't do any good to lose your head," Jessie warned.

"Lose my head! What if I lose Adriane? There's no telling what might happen to her, if she starts asking around about her father, stirring up trouble!"

"But slow down, Greg, that's what I'm saying. You can't just rush off in the middle of the night. You've got to stay around, at least until morning. Even in broad daylight, you won't be able to take the regular road to White Mule; you're a wanted man now. You'll have to take the long way around, across country, and it's hard country, where trees seem to grow out of the solid rock walls that hem them in. And you'll never be able to take a breath of rest, either, 'cause you'll be getting into Quaid Ruther's country!" Jessie pleaded earnestly. "So please, Greg, stick around and help us round up the cattle. Then get some rest, think over what's best, and maybe hide out until we get you cleared. Okay, Greg? *Greg?*"

Nehalem was gone.

A moment before, he'd been standing at the edge of the clearing. Jessie dashed to the spot, catching a slight ripple of foliage, a soft rustle of brush beyond, as the only indications of his departing presence. "I don't like it!" she called after him. If Greg Nehalem heard her, he didn't acknowledge, but swiftly faded, invisible and silent, into the enshrouding night darkness.

111

★

Chapter 8

Around noon of the following day, the shipping herd got on its belated way to the Houston stockyards. Jessie, feeling Moss could handle the drive as trail boss, and assuring him that she'd rejoin the drive in a day or so, rode with Ki for Monument in order to inform Fong Lu of the latest developments, and perhaps to learn of the whereabouts of Hacho Chown, Quaid Ruther, and Lieutenant Wolcott.

Naturally, she and Ki did not wish to have Hacho Chown, Quaid Ruther, or Lieutenant Wolcott learn of their whereabouts. So, arriving in Monument, they approached the livery by a circuitous back-alley route and, walking to Fong Lu's laundry, kept to the crowded sections of the boardwalk so as to lessen the risk of being spotted. Carefully they peered into the front window of the laundry before entering. But there was no one inside other than Fong Lu himself. And he, when they entered, swiftly whisked them behind the counter and back of the curtain, where there would be less chance of them being glimpsed by passersby or customers.

It did not take Jessie long to tell Fong Lu of

113

the surprise attack by Chown and his rustling gang, her narrow escape with Nehalem, and his subsequent vanishing.

"He should've stayed put here like I told him," Fong Lu said, shaking his head. "That is the trouble with some young men. They think with their— er, their hearts instead of their heads. You believe Nehalem is going to White Mule?"

"I'm sure of it, Fong Lu," Jessie answered. "What bothers me is that he might very well tie into Chown, and quite likely Quaid Ruther as well, there."

"I don't wish them or this Lieutenant Wolcott to catch up with him," Fong Lu admitted, glancing nervously out through the curtain. "Not now, but later I've no doubt he will welcome a chance to fight any or all of them. And so would I. I live for the day when they can give me news of my countrymen. And you? Will you be heading for White Mule?"

"First I want to meet with this Tobias Pembroke," Jessie said grimly, "to size him up, see where he fits in and—"

"Bluecoats!" Fong Lu hissed, gesturing streetward.

Peering with Fong Lu through the curtain, Jessie and Ki saw five troopers just dismounting in front of the laundry, tying their horses to the hitchpost. Lieutenant Wolcott was not in sight; his absence did not make them feel any better, for even without him there was the possibility that the troopers might recognize them as having been visitors at Fort Younger. Hastily Fong Lu ushered Jessie and

Ki through the back to the rear door; they slipped out of the laundry and headed for the livery where they had left their horses.

"I don't trust Wolcott," Jessie murmured as they headed swiftly along the alley-like side street that passed behind the livery. "I'd sure like to know where he is right now."

Making sure they weren't seen, they went around to the front of the livery and entered through the wide stable doorway, stepping into the gloom, with its stamping horses and the smells of hay and sweat and fresh droppings. The hostler sat in his cramped office, feet on his desk. Even from that distance, they could see that his face was pale. He watched them enter but made no move to rise, and Jessie's sixth sense began to work as she saw the hostler's wide, staring eyes. The man was wetting his lips now. A thin thread of tension flashed along her nerves. Up ahead she saw her grulla mare and Ki's moro gelding in adjoining stalls. Ki seemed to sense the unseen danger, too, for he slowed his pace.

Now their eyes were becoming accustomed to the gloom. Just as Jessie was about to turn so her back would be to the wall, a commanding voice cut out of the shadows from behind a pile of sacked grain.

"Hands up, Miss Starbuck! You, too, Ki! You are both under arrest for aiding and abetting in the escape of a U.S. Army prisoner!"

The voice had come from behind them, and Jessie knew without turning that it had to be that of Lieutenant Wolcott. Evidently he had been hiding there to cover them when they entered. The hostler had known he was there, but was powerless to interfere with a military arrest—not that the old bastard would've had the backbone to object anyway, Jessie thought.

Hands raised shoulder-high, she and Ki turned slowly. Ki, taking his cues from Jessie, showed no signs of defiance. Under other circumstances, Jessie might have tried to battle her way out of the trap, but she had no wish to fight an Army officer and run the risk of killing the man. She had little use for Wolcott, but, after all, he did wear the blue of a U.S. Army lieutenant.

Wolcott did not look as polished as he had that day at Fort Younger or, for that matter, as he had when he'd visited the Bar-B-Bar. Now more than ever his face appeared haggard, his uniform unpressed and his boots muddy. Nevertheless he still had a certain underlying dignity.

"What's the meaning of this?" Jessie demanded, stalling for time, her mind busy with the thought of escape. "Your charges are scurrilous! And you've got no authority to train a gun on us, no authority at all!"

"You helped Nehalem escape!"

"So Nehalem has outwitted you, is that it?" Jessie snapped back, evading the trap she knew Wolcott had set for her.

"I see you won't admit you knew that," the lieutenant said. "That'll come in time. Now I'll call my troopers and have you escorted to jail and then continue my search for Nehalem. I'm sure he's in this area, and I intend to find him. Next time, I'll have the pleasure of escorting all three of you to the Fort Brown stockade!"

Jessie realized that once the troopers were called, she and Ki would have no chance. Now was the time to act. She stiffened, and she noted that Ki shot her a sidelong glance, as if to anticipate her thoughts.

"I dispersed my troopers in plain sight," Wolcott said, evidently proud of his strategy. "I intended to give you a false sense of security, and it worked. You see, Miss Starbuck, the Academy makes an officer. Nehalem and civilians like you do not have that privilege, and therefore I've an unfair advantage over you."

There was a mocking tone in the lieutenant's voice. He was about to turn and yell for his troopers—the moment Jessie was counting on—but before Wolcott could execute his intention, a thick-set, ruddy figure entered the wide doorway— a man both Jessie and Ki instantly recognized as Quaid Ruther.

"Good work," Ruther exclaimed, a vicious smile of triumph stretching his lips. "How'd you catch 'em?"

Wolcott quickly told the teamster how he had captured Jessie and Ki, concluding with. "As soon as I take these prisoners to jail, we'll continue scouring this area for Nehalem."

"Let me haul Miz Starbuck and her sidekick to the jug," Ruther suggested craftily. "You don't want to lose any time."

For a moment the lieutenant weighed the wisdom of this. "Don't trust these two alone," he said finally. "Are your men nearby?

For an answer Ruther turned and whistled. Immediately three heavily armed gunmen stepped into the stable—one of them, Jessie noticed, being the black-haired Hacho Chown, still clad in his greasy buckskins. Smugly Ruther drawled, "Y'see? My men are never far away."

"You take over these prisoners, then," Wolcott declared as though it were an official order. "They are Army prisoners, though, so see that no harm comes to them."

"Perish the thought," Ruther replied piously.

And for the first time Jessie began to get a clue to Lieutenant Dunton Wolcott's character. Wolcott had the natural suspicion of most Academy graduates toward officers who had risen from the ranks, hence his ready acceptance of Nehalem's guilt and the assumption that she, Jessie, and Ki had helped some way in the escape. His vanity would not let him believe that Nehalem could have made the break unaided. So, all told, Jessie wondered if perhaps the young officer was merely overzealous and not in league with Ruther, as she'd first suspected. On the other hand, nothing had cleared Wolcott of being in cahoots . . .

The revolvers of Ruther's three gunhawks were brought to bear on Jessie and Ki. Inside the small office, the hostler had taken his feet off the desk now and was standing up, licking his lips; he definitely wanted no part in this trouble, but stood watching silently from the doorway.

Lieutenant Wolcott had holstered his pistol and was now running toward the laundry, shouting for his troopers. Bystanders on the boardwalk turned to gawk as the troopers hurriedly exited the laundry and began collecting around their superior officer, all seemingly talking at the same time about the same thing: where the elusive escapee Nehalem might be found.

Jessie, standing with Ki under the guns of Ruther and his henchmen, knew with sinking heart that should they try to make a break, it would very quickly involve those troopers—and if any of them were wounded or killed, Nehalem would very likely never be able to clear his record. After all, the troopers were merely following orders. The War Department would take the view that Nehalem should never have tried to escape, that the wheels of military justice would have turned and eventually brought about his freedom.

Ruther seemed to be reading Jessie's thoughts. "It looks like your li'l game is over, eh? Saddle your horses. We're gonna make sure you never have *another* game, bitch!"

Without a word, Jessie and Ki walked to their mounts, Ruther and his men fanning out across the stable barn so as to have them constantly under their guns. It was plain to Jessie that Ruther had no intention of taking them to jail; they would be taken out and shot. Ruther would then be able to tell Wolcott that they had tried to run for it. It was that basic—basic as death.

As they reached for their saddles on the pegs, Jessie had a second to whisper encouragement to Ki: "Watch me. We've got to make our break in here."

Used to danger as they were, they went about the business of saddling with no outward show of emotions, but feeling they might have one slim break developing in their favor: So far they had not been disarmed, Ruther no doubt figuring to let them get into the saddle and then shoot them down.

As if echoing their thoughts, Ruther turned and yelled an order to the hostler: "Go buy y'self a drink!"

The hostler hesitated. "But I oughter stay here!"

"Buy a drink!"

The hostler scurried out, never looking back.

"We don't want no witnesses, Miz Starbuck, do we?" Ruther purred. "Now, you two mount up, and be fast about it!"

It was obvious what he intended to do. He would let them ride toward the door, but before they reached it, they'd be shot to death. The horses would then stampede in the excitement, and Ruther's story would be accepted by the law. Two military prisoners had tried to make a break and had died in the attempt. Well, to hell with that!

Jessie, backing her grulla out of the stall, suddenly smote the mare on the rump with the flat of her hand. She jumped back into the shelter of the stall then, yelling for Ki to do the same. Ki needed no prompting; even as Jessie shouted, he was slapping his moro into action. Instantly, revolvers opened fire from Ruther and his men, who were forced to leap aside in order to escape the plunging horses, which were hurtling out into the middle of the stable, yellow teeth bared.

120

Deliberately Jessie showed herself, to draw fire away from the two horses. As bullets sang her way, she dropped the hammer on her own pistol. One of Ruther's men doubled up and pitched forward on his face, his weapon exploding into the ground. Ruther stepped aside from Ki's moro gelding and raised his gun to bear on Jessie. At that instant, an avalanche of frenzied horseflesh bore down on him. Jessie's grulla, whinnying shrilly, eyes dilated, raised on its hind legs, forefeet pawing the air. Ruther threw himself to one side and had to roll over and over, dropping his revolver in order to keep from being smashed by those slashing hoofs.

Ki's wrist-whipped *shuriken* nailed a gunman upright against the far wall. The man stood rigid for a moment, then collapsed. Hacho Chown dove into an empty stall to avoid the blasts from Jessie's pistol and the silent death from Ki's stabbing weapons.

There were shouts from the street as men raced for the stable.

"Let's make a run for it!" Jessie cried as she vaulted into the saddle. Ki had his moro's reins, and now he hit leather and followed Jessie's lead through the doorway. Shots from Hacho Chown's revolver, and then Ruther's as he retrieved his gun, whistled past their heads as they cleared the stable. Now the collecting crowd outside split in two as Jessie and Ki galloped toward them. Somebody fired a rifle at the two of them, but the shot went wild. Ruther's strident voice came to them dimly as they angled onto the main street and raced southward out of town.

"They're coming hard!" Ki shouted, indicating behind him.

Indeed, glancing back, Jessie saw a rising dust cloud and the flash of sabers in the sunlight. Lieutenant Wolcott had ordered his troopers a-saddle at the first inkling of trouble, and they were scrambling to obey, already nosing their horses in pursuit.

Let them, Jessie thought angrily, as she and Ki bent over their horses' withers and the animals chewed up ground. Shots snarled after them, but the swaying riders behind—a mix of troopers and Ruther's gunmen—couldn't aim effectively, their bullets off-target, high and wild. Jessie didn't bother to return the fire. It would be nip and tuck all the way, just concentrating on the race ahead.

The earth blurred under pounding hoofs. The rolling beat of pursuing horses echoed loud and thundering in their ears, the fusillade of lead buzzing close by their heads. To their left was the Colorado River, with flat banks and not much cover and a whole lot of open water, a sure cure for living. To their right rose the slopes in the inland hills, this side of which were bathed in shadows due to the angle of the setting sun, now low on the western horizon. No question which way to head; Jessie and Ki angled off the road for the hills, able to see the black maw of a pass, like a thin canyon, from which a hoof-trampled trail or cowpath led, connecting to the main wagon road.

Just before they reached the hills, they crossed

an expanse of sand, their horses' hooves churning up a great cloud of dust. As Jessie glanced back, she saw that their pursuers were screened by the dust cloud. That, she hoped, would work in their favor. Gesturing to Ki, she turned, with him following, into the canyon, which was grown high with oaks, and then reined in. They sat their winded horses, sheltered from the flats by a protecting shoulder of rock. They could hear the pound of the chasing horses as they swept nearer, then on past—

No! The riders reined in. Wolcott and Ruther confabbed . . .

"Shit!" Jessie exclaimed angrily, as she heard the riders veer into the canyon. Launching their horses into full run again, she and Ki could plainly hear the onrushing riders plunging after them. Urging their mounts to greater speed, she and Ki dashed along the bed of the canyon, the increasingly towering walls on either side of them echoing as the pursuers swept after them along the rutted trail. The chase continued, the canyon gradually rising and blending into the foothills and opening into a draw. Beyond, a wide, rock-strewn plateau extended to another maze of shadowy ridges and canyons. Naked of trees, the plateau gleamed under the dazzle of sunset, which made brilliant diamonds of the stones that littered their path.

The two rode hard across the flat. The only sounds were the deep panting of the horses and their drumming strides against the rocky soil—and the faint rataplan of hoofbeats coming after them.

Reaching the edge of the plateau, Jessie and Ki began skirting a twisted ravine. Still frantic to throw Wolcott and Ruther off their trail, they swung onto a barely visible track at a dead run. Another canyon embraced them, shrinking to a sinuous gorge of solid stone that reverberated with their passage. Ki slowed his horse and motioned Jessie to do the same. Their huffing mounts were glad to oblige. They moved along the granite floor, their easy lope giving off very little noise that could be traced. Behind, the sounds of galloping horses echoed off the rock as Wolcott and his troopers and Ruther and his gunmen entered the canyon.

"*Still* haven't lost them!" Ki growled, glancing back.

"Wait," Jessie said. "Listen! I don't know, but . . ."

Tensing, they strained to catch what Jessie thought she might be hearing. Then, from ahead, faint at first, but growing swiftly, rose a deep, earth-trembling roar. Still riding at a loping pace, they became increasingly alarmed the farther they went along the snaky gorge. But they couldn't stop or go back because of the pursuing riders, and they couldn't turn aside because of the steep slopes and flanking boulders on both edges. They could only continue heading toward the rolling, pounding, fast-approaching tumult.

A few rags of clouds shuttled across the sun-setting carmine glare, blown by a rush of wind from the north. They caught the crimson glow, and as the hellfire blaze pierced the gorge, the duo rounded a sharp bend and faced a looming herd of cattle. Hastily they reined in, aghast at the sight of this brown wall bearing down on them, heads tossing, eyes rolling, horns clacking, all squeezed within the narrow gully. It was being driven at a rapid clip by punchers silhouetted merely as figures against the glarish sky, their prodding shouts lifting above the drumming beat of hooves. A little in front trotted one curly-horned, wall-eyed steer that seemed to be the leader.

"I know that brute!" Ki shouted. "These're Bar-B-Bar cattle!"

"The Bryces'?" Jessie yelled, appalled. "Y'mean this's the shipping herd? Christ, whatever it is, back! Quick!"

Her voice was drowned in the deafening roar. Jessie and Ki wrenched their horses around to head back the way they'd come, Ki's moro kicking and plunging, Jessie's grulla dancing, ears laid back and eyes wild.

Fear was in the air, fear of this mass of flesh closing inexorably, no more to be halted than a tornado. To yell and wave would be futile; to shoot would be like damming a flood with loose rocks, and could easily result in panic, spooking the steers into stampeding in the only direction they could go— straight ahead.

The shadowy trail blurred under their horses, their pace too swift for talk, and none was needed. Each could sense the tension and dread in the other, as they galloped around another tight curve, and surged directly toward the oncoming troopers and gunslingers.

Wolcott and Ruther and their men were caught

by surprise, but not so much that they didn't react. Predictably, they spurred their horses on, whooping with certain victory, their weapons spurting flame and lead. At such dead-on range, Jessie and Ki should have been riddled, but in firing from speeding horses into dusky shadows, the pursuers' aim proved inaccurate. Despite bullets ricocheting uncomfortably close, Jessie and Ki continued their suicidal charge, figuring their only chance was to somehow break through the line of shooters and return to the plateau.

And then the herd came lumbering around the curve.

The gorge abruptly erupted in howling, rattling confusion, troopers and gunmen alike shouting in shock and fear, trying to check their horses and spin them about. Some went down as their horses slipped and fell on the shale. Others windmilled arms and hats in a vain attempt to stop the front. Still others, the really stupid ones, turned their fire from the two riders to the crowding steers beyond.

The cattle spooked. Lowing and snorting, they began picking up speed, and as one would stumble or drop with a bullet, the others would leap the barrier and stream on even faster. More gunfire peppered the advancing herd as the troopers and gunmen splintered frenziedly, a few retreating, most of them still attempting to stave off the stampede.

Jessie, caught in between along with Ki, felt the curly-horned leader brush past her, bellowing, with other steers thronging right behind. It was almost more than she could do to maneuver her horse out of their path. Ki, spotting her predicament, swung his moro in an arc to intercept her, as the rush of steers surged perilously around both of them in an increasing tide. The shoving melee flung him back as easily as a baby; he reeled, tilting far off balance, and the flinty tip of a longhorn snagged his jacket, gouging a burning furrow diagonally across his side and back. It was Ki then who would have lost control, had not Jessie swerved alongside and grabbed the cheek strap of his horse's bridle, pulling the animal around in line with the maddened herd.

They were swept along shoulder-to-shoulder with the steers, shoulder-to-shoulder with sudden death, but at least they were going in the right direction. Wolcott, Ruther, the troopers and gunmen were not. Men fell, horses tripped, and the stampede crushed them in its relentless pressure, trampling and slashing them under sharp hooves. The agonizing cries of the injured and dying were faint in the overwhelming, thunderous maelstrom.

And the avalanche of beef rolled implacably on toward the plateau, sunset glinting on tossing backs and piercing horns. Carried along in the hemming current, Jessie and Ki could hear the bellowing of frightened animals and the pounding of hooves drumming the stony trail. This was no place for a poor rider, or a coward.

The gorge widened into the short stretch of canyon, and from the canyon the herd funneled out, spreading across the plateau. Ki angled for the narrow crevice at one side of the canyon mouth, and Jessie followed, slumped in her saddle. The herd kept plummeting past in a swirl of dust and horns and hooves, not a dozen yards from the spot where they hunkered.

Eventually the drag drained through, the Bar-B-Bar crew behind them yelling and cursing as they tried to stem the runaway.

"Well, no question we got away from Wolcott, Ruther, and their bunch," Ki remarked with a sigh; then he added somewhat disgustedly, "But what a way to do it. Of all the crazy coincidences! Moss and that poor crew of his will never turn those cows, Jessie. We were supposed to be helping them, but believe me, by morning, those cows will be scattered from hell to breakfast out there in the breaks."

"Oh, maybe not. The herd shouldn't run too long," Jessie said, not fully believing it herself. "In any case, what's done is done. I see Moss over there . . . I guess we better fess up and go help gather in the fool cattle."

★

Chapter 9

Early the next morning, Jessie and Ki packed up
and left the Bar-B-Bar ranch for Houston. In
the afternoon, they crossed the Brazos and rode
through the flat Gulf plains, following a dirt wagon
road past wide fields of cotton. The wet wind from
the mighty Gulf touched them, and the heat was
like a steam bath.

When finally they reached Houston, evening was
at hand, the low sun sending its spreading rays in
golden splendor across Buffalo Bayou. Wagons and
saddle horses blocked the cobbled streets. Work-
men and a mixed crowd of passersby thronged the
sidewalks, and the street lamps and lights in the
saloons, restaurants, and residences were being
lit. The fast-growing port city pulsed with the
beat of humanity—with tradesmen serving the
inhabitants, sailors resting after long voyages,
ranchers and cowboys who had driven herds to
market, and gamblers and painted women and
thieves and worse rascals preying on decent folk.

Familiar with Houston, Jessie and Ki stopped at
a particular livery—Pete's Stable—confident that
their horses would be well tended to. Then they

walked toward the center of the city. Heedless and hurrying pedestrians bumped into them, and they had to dodge drays and hansom cabs as they crossed the streets. Entering the large restaurant and barroom known as Tony's Metropolis, they joined other diners at one of the long group tables, while aproned waiters bustled about serving platters of barbecued beef, pork, and mutton, salvers of steaming corn roasted in the husk, brimming bowls of chile colorado in fat, plates of chile relleno with crisp tortillas, and bottomless carafes of hearty red wine. Being ravenous, Ki gorged, washing down food with drafts of wine. Jessie ate sparingly, and when she was done, she got up and went over to the headwaiter, who was keeping an eye on things near the entrance.

"Excuse me," she said. "By any chance have you heard of a Houston businessman by name of Pembroke?"

"Pembroke? What's his first name?" The headwaiter turned away with a quick nod to speak to a waiter about the pastry tray.

When he came back, Jessie replied, "Tobias."

"Tobias who?"

"Now, wait a minute. I asked if you knew of Pembroke."

"Oh, yeah, yeah. Huh. Pembroke. I've heard the handle. Why don't you look in the city directory? The boss has one in his office."

The directory was a help. It listed Tobias Pembroke. Jessie quickly memorized the information and rejoined Ki.

"Any luck?" Ki asked.

"Interesting. Pembroke is a manufacturer and has a factory on Front Street. Let's sleep over and start on Pembroke in the morning."

They spent the night at the Corinthian Hotel and were up and had breakfasted at an early hour. They picked up their horses and rode the miles to Pembroke's factory, a long building made of red bricks sooted by the smoke from its big stacks. It was set off by itself in a large lot down by the waterfront. The firm had a private railroad siding on which stood several cars. The offices were in a smaller, adjoining structure, on the roof of which was propped a sign reading, "PEMBROKE & CO. Mfr. of Gunpowders, Fireworks, Matches, Sulphuric Acid. Wholesale Only."

Workers were arriving and pouring in through the factory gates. Jessie and Ki stayed back out of the way, across the street.

"There he is," Jessie said.

An equipage drove up and stopped before the office. The Spanish-looking man, whom the desk clerk in Monument had identified as Luis Gutierrez, jumped down and obsequiously assisted Tobias Pembroke to the walk. Pembroke was wearing a derby hat, kid gloves, and a gray checked cassimere suit with a diamond stickpin in his necktie, and he was carrying a malaca walking stick with a jeweled head.

"He sure gets duded up fit to kill," Ki observed.

Gutierrez, clad in the same plain outfit in which Jessie had seen him before, opened the office door for Pembroke and then followed him inside.

Jessie and Ki waited until the door had closed behind Gutierrez, and then crossed the street at a swift pace. Now more than ever Jessie could not fathom what Pembroke's game could be, attacking the farmers living in the hills outside Monument. Here in the broad daylight of the bustling city, it was hard to believe that the elegant proprietor of the powder plant had any connection with Quaid Ruther, Hacho Chown, and the roster of death that she and Ki had come upon.

Entering the Pembroke & Co. office, they found themselves in a square anteroom. There were chairs lining one side, pictures on the cream-colored walls, an umbrella stand, a coatrack, and a desk at which a young man sat watching them as they came in. Behind the young clerk on guard were two oak doors. On the one on the left was painted "MR. PEMBROKE. PRIVATE." The other was marked "OFFICES."

The clerk smiled. "Good morning. May I help you?"

"Tell Mr. Pembroke that Miss Jessica Starbuck is here to see him."

"Do you have an appointment, Miss Starbuck?"

"No, but he'll want to see me."

"I'm sorry, Mr. Pembroke's terribly busy this morn—"

"Tell him," Ki cut in, leaning on the desk. "Now."

The clerk looked at Ki looking at him, cleared his throat, rose from his desk, and went to the left-hand door. He tapped hesitantly. From the other side, Pembroke's sharp voice responded with an irritated ring: "Yes? Yes, what is it?" The clerk stood at attention. "Mist' Pembroke, sir, there's a Miss Starbuck, Miss Jessica Starbuck, wishing to see you, sir." There was silence; Pembroke did not answer for a long moment. Then: "I'll be with Miss Starbuck in a bit. Have her wait."

It was but a brief wait until a bell tinkled and the clerk, now back at his desk, nodded to Jessie. "You may go in now, Miss Starbuck."

They went into Pembroke's private office, Ki shutting the door behind them. Here, there were more pictures and more chairs, another coatrack and umbrella stand, as well as a row of filing cabinets and filled bookcases. The centerpiece of the room was an ornately carved mahogany desk, behind which Pembroke was standing in polite deference to Jessie.

"Sit down, Miss Starbuck, sit down." Pembroke essayed a smile, the seams of his face deepening. Jessie took a chair close by the desk, and Pembroke appeared genuinely pleased, for now he could sit down. And he did so with a sigh, his paunch relaxing, hidden by the desk. Utterly ignoring Ki, he regarded Jessie quizzically. "Have we met before? You have a familiar look."

Jessie hedged. "I'm sure I'd remember if we had."

"Perhaps it was a picture of you in some newspaper. You're rather well known, especially in business circles, although I don't believe my company's had the honor of doing business with Starbuck before. What may I do for you?"

"I'll get right to the point," she began. "I'd like you to furnish five hundred barrels of gunpowder."

133

"My! Have you any particular type in mind?"

"It'll be used for breaching and such purposes, I gather. Whatever you recommend I'm sure will be fine."

Pembroke reached for the bell on his desk. "I'll have Twill—"

"Oh, no! Please don't ring for your clerk," Jessie touched his arm. "Y'see, this's for a cause."

"A cause?"

"Actually, they call theirs a liberation movement."

Pembroke gaped in shock. "Y'mean, a revolution?"

"I suppose." Jessie shrugged. "To be honest, the rights and wrongs of their fight mean exactly zero to me. I'm after the same thing you are, and that's profit. In this case, if the rebels win, they've pledged to negotiate a licensing agreement with a Starbuck mining subsidiary."

"My dear lady! There's a federal law against gunrunning!"

"Well, of course there is. That's why we need to handle our deal sub rosa, confidentially, just between us."

"What makes you think I'd do any such thing?"

"A cartridge manufacturer recommended you highly."

"What's the company?"

"Please don't ask," Jessie replied, putting respect in her voice, not wanting to antagonize Pembroke until she could discover just what he was up to at Monument. "My arrangement with them for cartridges is as confidential as the one I want with you for explosives. Surely you understand."

Pembroke lapsed silent, his expression less startled than calculating. Good, Jessie thought; he might be preparing to bite the bait. Offhand, she knew of half a dozen wars going on throughout the world. There were rebellions to the south, across the Mexican border and in South and Central America, and in Europe, and fighting in Asia and Africa. On the frontier were quarrels with Indians and between large bands of white men as well. Gunpowder was a coveted and vital necessity in all these disputes. Pembroke was in a position to make quick fortunes with his factory, and Jessie was betting that so long as he got his money, he didn't care where the powder went.

"Come, come," Jessie urged. "Are you interested or not?"

"I'm considering . . . But you're right, *periculum in mora*—there's danger in delay." Pembroke began to drum on the desk with two fingers of his left hand. One-two-three. One-two. "Since your rebels intend to use this powder for breaching and the like, I advise increasing the percentage of sulphur to speed up the rate of burning. It'll be close to a blasting powder, Miss Starbuck, in whatever quantity you need. I've every facility here for large output. As you may know, gunpowder is a mixture of charcoal, saltpeter, and sulphur. We make our own charcoal. The nitrate is imported, brought in ships to our own wharf. A cartel has got hold of most of the domestic sulphur supply and jacked

135

the price, but I expect to solve that problem before long. At the moment, I'll have to charge more per barrel."

"Very well. I'm prepared to pay cash on delivery."

Pembroke continued drumming his fingers on the desk. "Where can I contact you?"

"I can be reached through my Starbuck office here in Houston," Jessie replied, feeling a warning suddenly prickle up her spine. She was seated facing Pembroke, with Ki standing just behind her, and at their backs was a small inner door that led into the other offices. She hitched her chair around hastily, just in time to see the silent opening of that door. Luis Gutierrez and a stocky redheaded man entered, leveling large-caliber revolvers at her and Ki. Pembroke, she realized, must have signaled them with his tapping!

"What's the meaning of this?" she demanded, knowing full well what the meaning of this was. Both gunmen stared eagerly at her and Ki, hoping for an excuse, an order, raring to strike.

"I know all about you, you and your interference, from Ruther," Pembroke snapped at Jessie. "Guterriez! Get rid of these spies! That fool Ruther must've led them to me. *Humanum est errare*—to err is human, but he and Chown have damn near wrecked my plans. Why, they may well be working for the law!"

Jessie gave a surprised laugh. "Don't be silly! So that's what's eating you. You figure we're snooping for lawdogs. I told you, all I want is to make money."

136

"All the more reason! I wouldn't put it past you to warn those yokels against me, get them to sell out to you instead, so you get rich at my expense. No, you're too dangerous to risk alive." Pembroke waved a plump arm in a sudden burst of anger. "Take them out, Gutierrez! I want you to come back and tell me they're shot, and then we're leaving for the hills. *Hora fugit*—time flies. To win, we must strike hard and fast, and this time I'll go along so there will be no mistakes." His eyes bulged with icy coldness as he regarded Jessie for a last time. *"Pollice verso,"* he said, and put both thumbs down, the condemnation to death.

"Move!" Gutierrez snarled, stepping aside and gesturing with his revolver toward the inner doorway.

Jessie rose and headed for the open door, Ki moving a step behind with feigned docility. Gutierrez and his partner watched them smugly, Ki's dejection quite disarming them. Jessie passed between them, entering the office beyond; and as Ki passed between them, their gun muzzles followed his movement, the gunmen preparing to fall in behind.

Suddenly pivoting, Ki rammed the heel of his left palm in a *teisho* blow to the redhead's temple, fracturing the man's skull like an egg and driving shards of broken bone into his brain. The redhead went collapsing back into Pembroke's office, dead before he hit the floor. Simultaneously Ki rammed at Gutierrez with a right-armed *yoko-hija-ate*—sideways elbow smash—to cave in the dark man's ribs and stop his heart. But Gutierrez

137

was fast, damn fast, and despite being caught off-guard somewhat, he weaved aside enough to miss the worst of the blow, while swinging his pistol for a point-blank shot at Ki.

Jessie, having flattened to the floor the instant Ki attacked, rolled over and came up with her twin-shot derringer clutched in her right hand. Frantically she fired, her bullet creasing Gutierrez's shoulder but failing to stop him. He was distracted, though, and before she could trigger again, Ki dove across the short distance and struck Gutierrez in the chest with his extended left foot. His ferocious kick buckled Gutierrez, carrying him backward into the other office, the pistol firing with a deafening roar alongside Ki's ear.

From Pembroke's private office came a howl of rage and fright, and a mad scrambling for the door to the anteroom. The noises passed unheeded, as Gutierrez staggered back past Jessie and slammed into a desk in the other office, then smashed hard against the far wall. But he remained upright, leveling his revolver.

Ki swiveled away from the inner doorway. Gutierrez was thumbing the hammer of his single-action pistol when Ki snatched up the coatrack beside the door and flung it, spear-fashion, the brass rack slamming into Gutierrez's face. Again his pistol discharged, and again the bullet whispered by Ki's ear as it sped harmlessly past into Pembroke's office.

The shot was still reverberating when Ki, leaping after the coatrack, met Gutierrez stumbling toward him. He halted Gutierrez with a *yonhon nukite,* the stiffened tips of his fingers knifing into Gutierrez's throat and rupturing his trachea. With a raspy sigh, Gutierrez wilted and died.

"Thank God," Jessie said as she stood up, tremulous with relief.

"Thank Him after we get out of here," Ki replied. "Pembroke will be siccing a gun-heavy gang on us any second now."

Both the door to the anteroom and the main entrance door were wide open, indicating the haste with which Pembroke and the clerk had vamoosed. Just as swiftly, Jessie and Ki raced out of the building and across to their horses. Untying reins, they flung themselves into saddles and raked their mounts into full gallop, making fast time away from the powder factory.

"Where to?" Ki asked.

"White Mule! Pembroke spoke of heading for the hills, and I'll bet those hills must be somewhere around that place. Anyway, that's where Adriane, her father, and Greg Nehalem were all going."

They lost a few minutes as they paused at the hotel to pick up their gear and check out. Picking up speed then, they spent the day putting miles between themselves and Houston, before finally pulling up and turning off the wagon road. Evening was coming on, and they hunted a spot where they could rest a little while, knowing they would make better time in the long run if they didn't wear out themselves and their horses. There was a small wooded mound overlooking the road, and they made for it, hiding themselves and their mounts in the low growth . . .

Dawn woke Ki. The sun was gilding the eastern sky, and he rose and stretched. Jessie stirred uneasily in her sleep.

Ki felt refreshed. He took a drink of water from his canteen and scanned the road stretching for miles in either direction. Houston could be made out to the southeast as the morning breeze dispelled the haze from the bayou. Dust rolled in a large cloud over the road coming from the city, and he knew at once that a band of horsemen were heading toward them. He brought out field glasses and focused them. He did not have to look for long, and with a quick exclamation, he jumped over to shake Jessie awake.

"Get up, Jessie! Pembroke and company are coming."

Hidden from the roadway, they waited while the bunch neared the wooded mound. There was upward of a dozen riders, heavily armed with pistols, shotguns, and carbines, strung out behind Tobias Pembroke in his black leather riding rig. Pembroke stared at the mound while passing, but there was nothing to draw him or his men off the route. They kept going, dust roiling under trotting hooves as they disappeared over a low rise.

Jessie sighed. "I sure wish I knew where they were going.

"I'll settle for knowing where *we're* going," Ki responded. "Exactly where is White Mule anyway?"

"That should be easy for you to find out," Jessie said with a trace of sarcasm. "Remember how you found me and Greg? Well, since White Mule isn't where we are, you simply have to look where we aren't!"

★

Chapter 10

It was two days later when they finally emerged
from the sagebrush and sand, just south of the
cluster of wooden buildings known as White
Mule. Dusty, thirsty, and weary, they moved
slowly down a slanting hill toward the settlement. Entering White Mule, they first sta-
bled their tuckered horses at the livery, which
was about in the center of the line of buildings. Then they strolled slowly, sizing things up,
watching out for Ruther or Pembroke and their
crews.

"No sign of Adriane or Greg, either," Jessie
noted.

Once, apparently, people had considered White
Mule a promising location, a sort of crossroads for
area ranchers and farmers. But, Jessie observed,
the land hereabouts was as poor, the vegetation as
stunted and sparse, as the hill country where she
and Ki had been chased by Ruther's gang. In fact,
that whole barren section was not far away, kind
of sandwiched in between Monument to the east
and White Mule here on the west. Not surprisingly, White Mule had failed to thrive, and now

it was just another isolated settlement, more of a riffraff's hangout.

"Ki, nobody's going to tell us a thing here."

"Likely not, but it's worth a try. I'll check the bars."

"And a lady can always shop the general store," Jessie said, pointing across to a crude frame building, whose flyspecked window bore a sign reading "EMPORIUM * NEEDS OF EVERY TRADE, WHIMS OF EVERY NATURE."

They parted then, Ki angling for the nearest of two saloons. Entering, he hitched at the bar and drank a beer, trying to draw out conversations. But the saloon seemed to attract an itinerant bunch—drifters and saddle tramps who didn't know one another, much less anyone else, and made it clear to strangers that they preferred it that way.

The second saloon was a grubby hole that catered strictly to bleach-eyed jiggers tight of mouth and long on twist, who made it clear to strangers that they preferred strangers out the door. The beer at the first saloon had tasted like soap; the beer that was served him here foamed out slimy green. He left it untouched and ordered a whiskey.

"Whiskey it is." The rotund, red-nosed bartender put an unlabeled bottle and a shot glass on the counter, and let Ki pour his own. "Two bits."

Ki paid the inflated price and drank. A liquid torch flowed down his gullet and ignited a blackpowder charge in his stomach. He shuddered convulsively, gasping, "What the hell's in this?"

"A chaw of tobacco for blend, and red pepper squeezings for spice," the barman declared proudly. "There are some who swear this here whiskey o' mine is sweeter'n the bonded stuff." Now inclined to be sociable, he added, "Them's my reg'lar customers. I ain't seen you in before. Passing through?"

And that, of course, was the cue for the show to begin. "Yeah, just pulled in from o'er Austin way, hunting up an old saddle pard of mine, Bill Williams," Ki said genially. "Last I heard, he was teamstering for Ruther's freight outfit in through here. Know of it?"

"Sure do. Billy Williams, y'say?"

"Just Bill. My age, only heavier and bowlegged," Ki said. It was an easy lie to tell; Bill and Williams were dirt-common names, and every freight company had somebody who answered such a description. "He gets a mite loud when he drinks, and likes to swagger some."

"Oh, him! Excuse me, but he can be a powerful pain."

"That's Bill. Say, how do I find Ruther's headquarters?"

The barman scratched his chin. "That might take a heap of doing," he finally said, "trying to find where Ruther operates from."

"But I thought this's where he runs his wagons."

"It is, an' I seen plenty of 'em rolling through town, carrying heavy cargo one way, lots of Chinese the other. It's just that I ain't heard tell where any of it winds up, and believe me, if anyone knowed, it'd be me. The stuff I listen to, parked behind this bar! Why, I recollect this one gent—"

"Maybe some of the Chinese could tell me where to look."

"Maybe, if there were some around. But they're all being herded east somewheres, and I've yet to see any of 'em headin' back through here."

"East of here, eh?"

"Right. But ain't no man livin' knows that hill country well enough to figure an exact location. Only way would be to stumble onto Ruther, accidental like."

"How encouraging." Thanking the barman for his assistance, Ki walked back outside.

Jessie was waiting for him. "I bought a map of the area, though the storekeeper wasn't too sure how reliable it is," she explained. "But he recalled a girl answering Adriane's description. Fact is, she asked him if he knew her father, Oscar Bryce."

"Did he?"

"Vaguely. Bryce came through here a couple of months ago with a freighter load," Jessie answered. "Said he was hauling mining equipment for Quaid Ruther. That's the first and last the storekeep saw of him."

Ki frowned. "Seems like folks just up and vanish in those hills," he said, staring eastward at the shimmering rises in the late sun.

They ate supper that evening in the kitchen of a family who took in boarders. Afterward, they questioned the family about the surrounding country and studied Jessie's map for spots where they would be most likely to find Ruther's base of operations.

Next morning, they rode east into the hills. It was hazardous going, mile after mile through jagged arroyos, skirting boulders, pushing up through tangled scrub brush, exploring canyons marked as "possibility" on the map. At every vantage point, they would scan the countryside with field glasses. But they saw nothing suspicious.

As the morning lengthened, they entered a badland cut and scored by erosion, crossed and crisscrossed by a maze of gullies. Scaly ridges rose and twisted like giant saurians, and weird wind-chiseled shapes lifted above the cosmic chaos. At noon they rested beside a spring, whose water tasted acrid and smelled like rotten eggs, reminding them of the well water at that abandoned farmhouse they'd stopped at days before. They ate a meal of dried beef and biscuits, then pushed on.

"Ruther must've hidden his outfit in a gopher hole," Ki growled.

"There's over a hundred square miles of hill country where he could've taken those Chinese," Jessie admitted, "and no doubt where Pembroke must've been heading to meet up with him. We just have to keep on searching."

They moved farther into the hills. Wild scarps greeted them, pallid alkali slopes, steep breaks and sandy washes, troughed by knife-like ridges— an arid waste of limestone, gypsum, and shale, barren save for dry grasses and anemic brush. It was late afternoon when they crested a rise where, against all odds, a grove of trees was precariously clinging to life. Just as Ki was scanning

147

the surrounding area, before pouching his glasses, he caught a movement in the adjoining valley.

"You see something?" Jessie asked, noting the tension on his face.

Ki lowered his glasses and handed them to her. She looked where he indicated, then uttered a low gasp of surprise. There *was* movement over there—a group of Chinese coolies trotting down a slanting trail.

Exhilarated, they worked their way across a hogback. At last they reached a spot along a bouldered rimrock where they could look straight down into a small valley, surrounded on all sides by almost sheer limestone cliffs. The only way in or out appeared to be through a narrow draw, which was blocked by a huge gate of split logs. The gate was guarded by rifle-toting men—members of Ruther's crew, by the looks of them. More gunmen were posted like sentries around a cluster of crude log cabins, and by the mouths of two mine tunnels at the base of one cliff. Still more were patrolling a long line of Chinese coolies, who were wheeling out barrows heaped high with what seemed from this distance to be clay. Stripped to the waist, the coolies were pushing the barrows into the near end of a large building, whose roof sported a number of stovepipes that were belching fumes and steamy smoke—the source of the noxious odor that permeated the air even at this distance. Another line with empty barrows was exiting the building and returning to the mine. Parked alongside the building were three empty freight wagons, similar to the one Ruther had at Fort Younger; a fourth wagon was being filled with large burlap bags, like feed sacks, which other Chinese were carrying out from the far end of the building.

It was a weird sight, for at this distance no sound could be heard. It seemed as if those workers down there were gnomes, scurrying around with desperate energy.

"Limestone, gypsum . . . Of course, it all fits," Jessie murmured grimly, handing the glasses back to Ki. "We've found it. We've found our answer."

Using the glasses again, Ki said, "We've found more than that." He pointed to the line of coolies emerging from the tunnels. "Nehalem and Fong Lu."

"*What?*" Snatching back the glasses, Jessie focused in on the line. It was harder to identify young Fong Lu among the other Chinese, but there was no mistaking the tall ex-lieutenant. Like the rest of the line, they were struggling to push loaded barrows toward the large, smoke-wreathed building. As Jessie watched, she saw the man behind Nehalem accidently bump him with his barrow; Nehalem tripped and fell to the ground, whereupon one of the gunmen kicked him unmercifully until he managed to stagger erect. She had started to tell Ki about the brutalization, when she caught a glimpse of three more Anglos farther back in the line. They were just emerging with wheelbarrows from the tunnel, their shirts hanging in tatters, their pants ripped and stained—blue pants, with a gold stripe down each leg. "Troopers!" she gasped. "There's Wolcott, Lieutenant Wolcott and two of his squad!"

"They must've run into a trap," Ki said grimly.

Jessie nodded. It was a good guess that, first, Fong Lu had decided to help Nehalem and left Monument to join him. Second, Nehalem had inquired for Adriane at White Mule, which somehow resulted in a tangle with Ruther's gang. And third, Lieutenant Wolcott and his squad had been pursuing Nehalem, and had also been waylaid and captured.

"Let's get closer," Jessie said.

"It's risky."

"It's the only way, Ki. We've got to try and figure how to rescue Greg, Fong Lu, and those troopers. And I've a hunch that Adriane and her father are prisoners down there, too."

Ki knew that further argument was useless once Jessie made up her mind. After tethering their horses in a relatively grassy niche, they began a cautious descent. Dizzy heights held no terror for them, and their practiced eyes picked out rock formations that slanted down the cliff, outcroppings, ledges, an occasional dwarf pine. All these would be stepping stones on that treacherous descent into the valley. Any slip, a slight miscalculation, and they would go plunging to their death.

As they worked down the cliff, they kept watch on the gunmen guarding the Chinese, who continued in a constant stream to trundle wheelbarrows mounded with clay from the mine to the building—in which there must be furnaces, Jessie said; regenerative furnaces for beneficiation. To which Ki said nothing, only cursed under his breath and scanned the sides of the valley for signs of gunmen posted as lookouts.

Nearly an hour later they had descended halfway down the cliff. Now, as the sun dipped below the ragged rim of the hills, evening shadows were beginning to cast their purple across the west side of the valley. And, by now, Ki had carefully spotted all the guard positions—including that of a gunman standing almost directly below them, on a rocky shelf a few feet above the valley floor.

Once, Jessie nearly fell, and it was a dwarf pine growing out of a rocky wall that saved her life. Her eager fingers grasped this as she pulled herself back to a rocky outcrop to rest a moment. Cold sweat bathed her body, for like Ki, she feared that this sudden movement might have been seen by those below. But so far there was no indication that they had been observed. Wiping her hands on her denims, she began to move down with Ki once more.

They hesitated at the point where they were about ten feet above the guard on the rocky shelf. Clearly the gunman never expected anyone to drop down from above; his attention was centered on the workers, his job evidently to kill any Chinese who attempted a break for freedom. Neither Ruther nor Pembroke could afford to have anyone escape from here and live to blab about it.

Ki paused, gauging his leap, then sprang down on the big-hatted guard. He felt the shock of the gunman's shoulder against his chest as they crashed together. The rifle was knocked aside. The powerfully built man writhed as Ki's strong left

151

arm encircled his neck, choking off the scream that was fighting to get past his lips. As they fell to the rocky shelf, Ki chopped his fist into the man's chest in a lethal heart punch. The guard went limp.

Jessie jumped down to the shelf then, while Ki watched to see if they had been discovered. Apparently the fight had gone unnoticed. The routine of this remote fortress seemed undisturbed. Whether it was or not, though, they couldn't stay here on this little ledge with the dead gunman.

They were just about to work down the path that led to the valley floor, when they heard the *whing* of a bullet ricocheting off the rock behind them. Stone shards stung their necks. An instant later came the crack of a rifle from a great distance. Snatching up the rifle at his feet, Ki tried to spot the marskman, who fired again. By now the valley was in confusion. Guards tore around, more appearing from the cabins, attempting to locate the trouble. Another slug sang over Jessie and Ki's heads as they dove flat on the rocky shelf. Now Ki spotted the hidden marskman. There were four spindly trees on the cliff above the canyon entrance. These had been stripped and bound together with cables, and a lookout house built on their tops.

Ki raised himself to his knees, took quick aim with the captured rifle, and fired. He saw the lookout fall forward to hang for a moment on the sill of his shelter. Then he described graceful arcs as he dropped spinning to the ground—but Ki failed to see this part, for now he was backed with Jessie against the cliff wall, hearing a familiar voice bellowing:

"There they are!"

It was Quaid Ruther, who had come out of the main building and was now indicating the trapped pair with a wave of his hands. His gunmen rushed forward. Some of the coolies, seizing a moment for escape, attempted to race for the gate at the entrance, only to be shot down before they had taken a dozen steps, adding to the confusion.

Ki levered the rifle for another shot, while Jessie had her pistol blazing in her hand. One of her slugs knocked a guard into a sprawling heap. Another suddenly doubled up and rolled on the ground, clutching a bullet-punctured chest. The guards stalled under the deadly fire. All was chaos in the valley—the yelling guards, the crack of guns, and the cries of the dying Chinese. Jessie spotted Hacho Chown in the melee, trying to rally the men for another charge. Ki, glimpsing the ponderous figure of Tobias Pembroke hovering inside a doorway, triggered a hasty shot with the rifle; the slug missed by a whisker, splintering the doorjamb and dumping Pembroke unceremoniously back on his butt.

It was Ki's last shot. Jessie's pistol, too, clicked empty.

The guards swarmed up the path to the ledge then, raging for vengeance. One gunman lunged with his rifle leveled as though to skewer Ki. Ki caught it, jerked, whirled, grappling with his attacker. He had a glimpse of burning eyes, a bearded face. A second man reared enormously on Ki's right, grappling for Jessie. She flung up her arm to fend off this other man's blow. It crashed through her effort, thudding against her skull. She felt herself falling. Then she felt nothing at all. Ki struggled to help her, but now three men were upon him, punching him, their weight pinning him flat and knocking out his wind. The barrel of a descending carbine cracked the side of his head. With a startled grunt, he blacked out . . .

★

Chapter 11

Jessie awoke with pain. Her head pulsed to a savage ache while she lay, eyes closed, gradually recovering consciousness. As her reviving wits labored to remember what had happened, she heard low murmurings of conversation echoing close around her. The sound pushed the fog back, and she opened her eyes.

A faint light threw wavering shadows on a low stone ceiling. Stirring, Jessie found herself in a bunk. She had the quick, groggy impression of solid rock walls and a heavy plank door. An iron-barred opening, like a little window, in the door. A kerosene lamp outside the door casting the faint light through the opening . . .

The droning talk had not ceased. Jessie turned her head and saw no one. Trying to sit up was an effort. She almost cried out at the pain hammering under her scalp, and she sunk back. Then she heard Ki say in a growly voice, as though speaking through clenched teeth:

"Easy, Jessie. Just lie there and rest."

She took his advice, waiting for her eyes to adjust to the darkness. Shifting, then, she saw Ki sitting with his back against the wall, gingerly fingering his split scalp. He was bare to the waist and showed signs of having been beaten cruelly. Sickened, she glanced away, and now made out the seated figures of Nehalem, Wolcott, and the two other troopers.

"Where . . . are we?" she managed.

"Down in the mine," Nehalem replied.

She swung her legs to the floor and sat on the edge of the bunk. The room swam dizzily. Her gunbelt and pistol were missing, but luckily she hadn't been searched or tied up, Ruther and Pembroke apparently having assumed she'd been left unarmed and defenseless. But a lot of good being able to spring her derringer did with nobody around to draw it on.

Nehalem came over and sat down beside her. "Sure sorry to see you. Ki's told us what happened," he said, and then he related how he and Fong Lu had been captured. They had arrived at White Mule and learned from the hostler at the livery that a girl answering Adriane's description had gone into the hills. Nehalem lost his temper and tried to choke further information from the hostler. Several of Ruther's gunmen, in town for supplies, heard the ruckus and upon investigation captured Nehalem and Fong Lu. "My temper is always gettin' me into trouble," Nehalem concluded ruefully.

"Where's Fong Lu?"

"In another of the cells, in with other Chinese. This whole mine tunnel serves like a holding pen for them poor bast—er, slave laborers."

"And Adriane?"

"Up on top, in one of them cabins. They killed

her pa," Nehalem said glumly. "Ruther told her it was an accident, that Mist' Bryce wanted to help some Chinese escape and got shot down by the guards."

Wolcott spoke up: "It was same as murder! Just like it was when they ambushed my squad, killed all but me an' Polk an' Johansen, here. I should've died, by all rights. Ruther was makin' a fool outta me from the first git-go."

"He's skunked a lot of folks," Nehalem said.

"I appreciate you not holding my idiocy against me, Greg. If nothing else, I've learned the hard way than an officer commissioned from the ranks is as good as any West Pointer—p'raps better." Sighing, he shook his head. "What I ain't learned, though, is what this's all about, what Ruther and that fat dude, Pembroke, are after."

"Sulphur," Jessie answered.

Nehalem glanced at her quizzically. "I don't get it."

"I didn't either, not at first," Jessie said. "I got my first suspicions when Ki and I were chased into these hills by Ruther's men. After we lost them, we took a breather at an abandoned farmhouse. The well water there smelled like rotten eggs, tasted that way, too, meaning it was sulphurous. And the ground under the topsoil was dull yellow, with brownish and blackish veins, also indicating high sulphur content. My suspicions were confirmed today, when I saw that this hill country is formed largely of limestone, gypsum, and bituminous shale, which are good signs of sulphur deposits."

"Y'mean, all this barren rangeland is settin' atop sulphur?"

"That's right, Greg. Somehow Pembroke learned of it and checked up, found it was so. He kept it quiet and sicced Quaid Ruther on Bryce and the other ranchers who own sections here, to kill them or ruin them by rustling their stock. Either way, Pembroke figures to pick up their properties cheap. I didn't find out what Pembroke is after, though, until we located him in Houston and learned he's a gunpowder manufacturer. He owns a big business and's making plenty of money, but aims to expand. Gunpowder's composed of saltpeter, which is potassium nitrate, of charcoal, and of sulphur. The sulphur is hard to get right now, and Pembroke can become a major supplier to himself and the general market by the mining and beneficiation—"

"Benny-what?" Wolcott blurted.

"It's like refining, or purifying. Like smelting is to gold."

"Oh, you mean that big contraption where we wheelbarrow the dirt," Nehalem said. "That thing that looks like a giant whiskey still."

Jessie nodded. "Very similar. It's called a Gill regenerative furnace, and employs the heat of combustion of sulphur to vaporize the remaining sulphur, which is recovered by condensation. Then the solid sulphur is bagged, and Ruther's wagons freight it out. Considering the money to be made, Ruther and Pembroke aren't the sort who'd worry over doing in a few folks."

"*Big* money?" Nehalem asked.

"A fortune. Sulphur is used not only for gunpowder, but in making matches, fireworks, medicines, bleaching compounds, and sulphuric acid."

"Adriane's rich, then!"

Ki laughed once, harshly. "Sure—if she lives."

"We've got to save her!"

"Greg," Jessie said, "first we have to save ourselves."

They all compared notes then, recalling what they could about the layout of the remote, fortresslike mine. But even this pooled information offered them no tangible plan.

"We've got to do something," Nehalem insisted.

"Now, don't go off half-cocked again," Wolcott cautioned. "It would solve nothing to kill ourselves."

Ki allowed a slow smile to spread across his face. "It might. It might just work . . ."

They agreed that they'd have to wait to strike until guards came by, so they sat huddled in the dark cave-like cell counting the hours that passed like years, while they made plans.

It was one of Wolcott's troopers who first heard the echoing bootsteps of approaching gunmen in the tunnel corridor. "They're coming," he whispered, glancing at Ki. "A couple of 'em, I think!"

Ki nodded. Then, loudly so that the men outside would hear, he said, "Greg! What's killing yourself going to gain?"

"I'll die anyway, here. And with them having Adriane in their filthy clutches . . . ! God knows what evil things they're doing to her!" Nehalem ended in a choking sob a mite overdramatic,

Jessie thought, listening as he went on: "Fong Lu gave me this secret deadly Oriental poison. One sip is all I need."

"Stop him, Wolcott!" Ki cried.

"What's going on in there?" one of the guards yelled through the door.

There was a moment of silence inside again. "I reckon you're right, Lieutenant," Wolcott said. "It's hopeless. We might as well all do it. I don't hanker to get starved and tortured to death. Here, gimme that poison bottle."

Nehalem was groaning now. He and Wolcott had moved to one side of the door, Ki and the two troopers to the other. Already they could hear a key rattling in the large iron-plated lock; gratingly, the door was unlatched, and as the door creaked open, the guards outside plunged into the cell. But before they realized the trick, an avalanche of human flesh smote them. Nehalem and Wolcott took the nearest guard, a burly hombre with a heavy brown beard. Ki and one of the troopers had the other guard, with Jessie and the second trooper jumping in to help. Clamping an armlock on the brown-bearded guard, Nehalem threw him heavily to the stone floor—

A shot rang out, deafening in the small enclosure.

And a shout: "Aw'ri'! Back! Back, you bastards, or I'll plug the bunch of you!"

In the doorway of the cell, leveling his smoking revolver at the prisoners, stood a third gunman—Hacho Chown.

The fighting stopped abruptly. Having no choice

but to obey Chown, the prisoners backed slowly, warily, deeper into the cell. Behind him stood another pair of gunmen; each gripped a revolver in his right hand, but one had hold of a glowing lantern in his left, while the other swung a ring of keys with his free hand.

Chown glared at the two downed guards. "Get up, you idjits. Get up and do what we were sent to do. Tie the Chink's and the floozie's hands behind 'em." He eyed Ki and Jessie then, adding with a malicious grin, "The boss wants to see you two."

Under the gun, the group stood still while Ki's arms were jerked behind his back and his wrists securely bound. Jessie's hands were likewise tied behind her with rope. Then they were prodded out of the cell. The gunman acting as turnkey shut and relocked the iron-bound cell door, and then he and the gunman with the lantern started along the tunnel corridor, followed by Chown, with the two downed guards falling in behind Jessie and Ki, angrily prodding them with their gun muzzles.

Stinking of smoke, sweat, and sulphur dust, the corridor was lined on both sides by locked cell doors, behind which could be heard the snorings, coughings, and moanings of the aged Chinese slaves who labored in the mine and wheeled the barrows of raw sulphur. At the head of the tunnel, the turnkey and the other gunman entered a small room, which evidently served as a sentry post. Chown continued on, leading the way up rickety wooden stairs of scaffolding that ascended the mine shaft. The staircase zigzagged back and

161

forth, cutting back on itself so that this, the fourth level, was directly below the second, and the third landing was directly above the top level.

On each level was another cell-like sentry post, although the only other one occupied was on the second level. There, the bored turnkey gestured obscenely at Ki as they passed. Ki ignored the insult and quietly tested the rope that bound him. It was tight and well knotted—but not tight or knotted enough. A slight, humorless smile creased his mouth as he twisted and flexed his wrists, sensing the weak points. The gunmen, having put their faith in the ropes restraining him, would be less watchful and cautious.

He relaxed then, feeling a bit more confident, as they trooped out of the mine into the open night air. Chown and the two gunmen guards led him and Jessie across the valley clearing, past a number of cabins filled with bunks. These were evidently the barracks where other guards slept and lounged during their off-duty hours. Farther up a gradual incline was a small log cabin, heavily guarded. Through its open door, Ki glimpsed powderkegs and stacks of cartridge cases; here was both the arsenal for the guards and the storeroom for explosives used in the mine. No wonder the cabin boasted so many guards.

They went up a dry creek bed that ran beside the arsenal, slanting down from the cabin nearest the big building where the sulphur was processed. Beside the big building a crew of Chinese worked beside a fifty-five-gallon drum of kerosene, filling lanterns used in the gloomy tunnels of the mine.

162

They stared at Jessie and Ki with expressionless almond eyes, their faces immobile as they bore their fate with the stoicism of their race.

Reaching the cabin nearest the building, Jessie and Ki were shoved through the doorway into an interior warmed by a fat potbellied stove. The door of the firebox was open, the blazing fire inside casting a flickering glow out over familiar faces: Quaid Ruther and Tobias Pembroke.

"Welcome," Pembroke said, gloating, a blocky shadow in front of the stove. "You've learned your first lesson, I believe. *Nemo me impune lacessit.* No one attacks me with impunity."

Ruther was less cordial in his greeting, snarling, "You almost ruined our plans! We had the stupid Chinese in the palms of our hands. You were going to interfere!"

"The Chinese aren't stupid," Jessie retorted, stalling desperately for time to figure a way out, a way to turn things around. "You tricked them into believing you, you must've!"

"Sure, we tricked them," Pembroke said. "We swore them to secrecy, promising them shares of the profits from the mine. With the money they'd make, they could return to China and be buried with their ancestors."

"But instead when you got them here, you imprisoned them," Jessie snapped. "When they died from your cruelty, there were always new slaves to take their places."

"We've had to use such methods, Miss Starbuck, because this deposit can't be mined profitably otherwise. If this were a surface deposit, as found

163

in the Aleutian Islands, the Sierra Nevada Mountains, Mexico, or Italy, we could mine it simply through open-pit, gophering, or room-and-pillar methods. But this is underground, and although the grade of ore is running around 35 percent, we must remain competitive. On the plus side, the deposits underlie this entire section of hill country. There must be enough to supply the whole United States, maybe the world!"

"If you can obtain title to the land hereabouts."

"Which we are, Miss Starbuck, are we not? Considering the profits, you can hardly expect me to care about the fate of some Oriental foreigners or a few hardscrabble ranchers."

"Or worry about you guys," Ruther added, and slashed the gun barrel of his pistol viciously down over Ki's head, sending Ki crumpling dazed and bloodied to the floor. *"Ki!"* Jessie cried and lunged forward, only to be restrained by Chown and the gunmen. As she struggled vainly in their grip, Ruther swore and demanded, "Lemme kill him, Toby! Gawd, what I owe this squint-eyes. Lemme plug him here 'n' now!"

Pembroke shook his head. "No, We'll let him live to see the wedding."

"What wedding?" Jessie asked warily.

"The fortune I'd have as the husband of the heiress to the Starbuck fortune would dwarf the money to be made in this sulphur mining. Why, I'd command American industry! I'd rival Gould and Vanderbilt. The world will point with envy to Tobias Algernon Pembroke. I'll settle wars and other great affairs. Not," he added smoothly as he faced Jessica, "that I'd wish to force a woman to become my bride."

"Don't worry," Jessie cried. "I wouldn't marry you under any circumstances."

"As I say, I wouldn't wish to force you. But you marry me, and Ki and the others stay alive. Refuse me, my sweet, and they die."

Jessie gasped, glancing with horror-filled eyes from Pembroke to Ruther to the hunched figure of Ki struggling to regain his feet.

"T'waz my idear, slut," Ruther sneered, "and a good'n it was, to make up for all the interference you two have caused. Personally, I hope you refuse, so that I can—" He ended his sentence by striking Ki again.

Again Ki slumped, blinding pain seeming to shatter his skull.

"Don't kill him!" Jessie screamed.

Instead, the two gunmen joined in, tackling Ki in a pile, grabbing his legs and tied arms and pounding him with their fists. Ki resisted, using elbow smashes, kicks, punches, his whole body as a weapon. But already weakened and groggy by the beating earlier, he could not hold them off. They smashed his ribs and battered his face and kept trying to break his bones with their heavy boots. Still Ki struggled, wishing he could resist completely and lay waste to these gunmen, and grimly enduring the pain as he battled to regain his feet.

"Don't kill him!" Jessie screamed, helpless in the grasp of Ruther and Pembroke. "No, don't! Let him go!"

The odds against Ki took their toll. Fists kept hammering, hammering, driving him to his knees. He buckled against the three men as they strove to keep him down. Then a well-aimed gun butt struck the back of his head, and again, harder, and Ki dropped flat on his face.

"Make up your mind, my sweet," Pembroke told Jessie. "Either you marry me willingly, or Ki dies, here'n now, followed by Nehalem, Fong Lu, and the bluecoats."

At a nod from Pembroke, Ruther cocked his revolver and stooped, to place the muzzle at Ki's temple. Jessie screamed in anguish as she tried to free herself from the clutches of Pembroke and Chown, who held her by her bound arms. To no avail. "How . . . how do I know you won't kill him, kill everyone, anyway?" she asked weakly.

"You have my word," Pembroke replied suavely.

Jessie nodded her aquiescence. Ruther straightened and holstered his revolver. Smirking, Pembroke ordered the two gunmen, "Take her in with that Adriane bitch, make her comfy." Without another word, she was led out through a side door into another room, and the door closed behind her. Pembroke nodded to Hacho Chown. "I think you can handle this bastard by his lonesome," he said, referring to Ki. "When you get him back to his cell, come back here. I reckon Ruther an' I will have more for you to do, then."

With Hacho Chown stabbing his revolver in his ribs, Ki was marched out of the cabin and back toward the mine. There was virulent hatred in Ki's eyes as he glared at Ruther. "Pembroke tricked her," he said.

"Natch'lly he did," Chown snickered. "You think we's fools?"

"Chown," Ki said, iron in his voice, "harm Miss Starbuck, and I'll come back. Living or dead, I swear I'll come back and get y'all for it."

Hacho Chown laughed caustically. "Never you mind, Chink. In a li'l while you won't have to worry about any female. Nobody has broken outta here, ever. The holes you slant-eyes are in are really remarkable."

Ki did not argue or give Chown an angry retort; instead, pursing his lips, he began freeing his wrists from the rope. Focusing all his concentration on the task, he purposely dislocated the bones of his wrists, then his hands, even his nimble fingers. Then, by merely twisting and stretching his ligaments and muscles, he began worming his limp, formless flesh through the encoiling bonds.

But he stopped short of letting them go altogether; the timing had to be just right before he dropped the rope, if he was to have any chance. There was no question that he was willing to take such a chance, though, no matter the odds. Pembroke had Jessie, had forced her into agreeing to be his slave. A slave no better off than the Chinese slaves he had digging his fortune in sulphur. The explosives magnate's greed was depthless, meaning his need was endless—need for slaves and more slaves. Slaves to replace those shot down or whipped to death, for those unequal to hard labor and a starvation diet . . .

Reaching the stairs at the mine shaft, Ki glanced down to the level below and noticed the turnkey there coming out of his sentry post. With him were two more gunmen toting Springfield Yergers. Then, as Ki crossed the top landing to the stairs, he leaned over the edge and saw, far beneath, the dim plane of the third level.

"A long drop, eh?" Chown smiled sarcastically.

Ki did not answer, not directly. He was looking straight ahead when he stiffened his body and let his eyes widen. At the same time he surreptitiously let the rope binding his hands slide through his fingertips and drop, falling slack to the landing, while in a voice that echoed through the dank mine, he shouted: "That turnkey!"

For just that instant, Hacho Chown's surprised attention was focused entirely on the turnkey below. "Whazzat—"

Snapping his bones back into place, Ki grabbed Chown by one arm, spinning him around in front. Chown yelled and tried to jam a boot against the stairs to stop himself. But Ki's weight was flung against him; they tottered together on the edge, and went off together, and Chown screamed.

It seemed an eternity of falling before they struck. Ki had jerked Chown beneath him, so it was Chown who took the full shock. Even then, Ki's body seemed to explode with pain, and he heard his own involuntary gasp. The rock walls spun around him as he fought to rise to his hands and knees. Chown moaned, stirred weakly, reached up to grab Ki. Ki caught his head and slammed it against the stone flooring. Chown collapsed, his head strangely revolting, somehow, gleaming faintly pale, and dead, against the dark blot of ground.

On the second landing, high above, the turnkey and two other guards had begun coming down toward Ki, their bullets ricocheting off stone as they opened fire. But it was dark down there, and their lantern only made a small circle of light directly above them—they were shooting blind. On the third landing, Ki rose to his feet, panting, shaking, and began fumbling for Chown's revolver, an old Starr .44, which had fallen with them and hit the landing a few feet away. He also retrieved a small hatchet that had dropped from Chown's belt.

Well, well. Hacho Chown. *El hacho*—the hatchet.

Now Ki knew who had murdered the desk clerk in Parumph.

Down on the fourth level, a turnkey and gunmen were already charging out of the sentry post there. Ki's first shot rocked the dank walls, sending down the guard carrying a lantern. Before the lantern spluttered out, Ki shot the turnkey and, in the darkness that descended, heard him scream and fall. He could hear the second-level turnkey and his men coming down, but they showed a reluctance natural under the circumstances, and he prayed for the time that would give him. Plunging down the steps to the fourth level, he began a desperate search of the dead turnkey for weapons and the ring of keys.

The second-level turnkey and his men had reached the third level now; one of them blurted out a vicious curse. Light from their lantern must have illuminated Chown's body. The gunman holding the lantern had turned down toward Ki now, and the lamplight caught the surprise in his eyes, and the understanding. "Evans! Panhardt! Look here at Hacho Chown!"

Ki's shot drowned him out. He fell forward, dropping the lantern. With a wild cry, the other gunman began firing, turning to stumble out of the circle of light cast by the lantern flickering in the stairway. Ki fired again, and the second man dropped. Panic-stricken, the turnkey began scrambling up the stairs. Ki triggered; the hammer clicked on an empty chamber. Discarding the useless revolver, Ki took aim with the hatchet. The turnkey was a running blot in the gloom above him. Ki's tomahawk-style toss sent the hatchet whirring end over end, striking the turnkey at the base of his neck, its sharp blade passing between the vertebrae, slicing his spinal cord and bringing his misspent life to an end without so much as a whimper.

Fearing that the gunshots might have roused the gunmen sleeping in the cabins outside, Ki hastened down the tunnel, unlocking the cell doors as swiftly as possible. Some were empty. Some contained a few, others a packed number of Chinese slave laborers. They—and Nehalem, Wolcott, and the troopers—all came out into the tunnel with vast disbelief. For them the idea of escape was long since a forlorn hope, yet here they were free of their cells, gathered about Ki, ready for any gamble.

When released, Fong Lu hugged Ki and then spoke to the growing numbers of his countrymen. "The guards are devils, tough and mean and without human feeling. They will fight, but they can be beaten—yes, those of us here can kill them all if we have weapons.

"And weapons you shall have," Ki said. "Check the dead gunmen on the landings, and empty the sentry posts on each level. But we must move fast and quietly, to get out of the mine before the other guards outside catch on and bottle us up in here."

Like a silent cyclone, the slaves surged up the staircase on padded feet. Outside, the night lay silent under the moon, without movement save for the routine pacing of the guards. Through the moonglow the slaves deployed, vengeful men, remembering endless abuses at the hands of these outlaws. A coyote wailed eerily from a nearby crest. And hard on the heels of that mournful ululation came the challenge of a guard.

"Halt! Who's there?"

"Devil and Sam Houston!" Lieutenant Wolcott's old Texican war cry rebounded from the hills, and he along with Nehalem and the troopers were running, dodging, while the Chinese were matching with a fiercely yelled charge of their own. Whirling to meet them, the half-asleep guards on night duty must in all truth have thought they were being attacked by demons seven feet tall and big as horses. They shrieked in one voice, reaching for their belted weapons. Not one was quick enough. The first assault was over in a matter of seconds.

171

And now the prisoners had many more weapons; half the Chinese had revolvers, and all possessed at least a knife.

But now other gunmen, many more gunmen, were pouring out of their cabins, their muzzles painting lurid patterns in the night. Guns began snarling, their bullets droning their unavailing way past weaving, moon-distorted slaves bidding for liberation, who answered in kind. Kill or be killed!

While the valley was erupting in battle, Ki scooped up the revolver of another dead gunman and started sprinting along the far wall of the large building. Suddenly he sprawled as his feet became tangled up in a pile of metal objects. He pulled himself to his feet and saw he had stumbled over lanterns. Nearby was the fifty-five-gallon kerosene drum perched on the edge of the dry creek bed. An ax was buried in the wood block beside the building. Prying the ax from the wood block, Ki hacked at the kerosene drum. A bullet slammed out of the darkness and drilled into the metal container; instantly a thin stream of kerosene sprayed out. Ki continued chopping at the drum, the blade finally cutting a gaping hole in its side. He widened it. Shouts were drawing closer, and he knew the guards had spotted him and the kerosene, which was cascading out now, pouring down the slanting creek bed, past the arsenal.

"Kill him! Shoot him!" The guards were in a shouting frenzy.

Doubling over, Ki escaped the hail of lead that stormed at him. Two guards with lanterns bore down on him, but Ruther's gunmen had to be careful in the gloom, for they had been shooting one another by mistake. This pair held their fire too long, and Ki shot one, and would have shot the other, but his gun, too, clicked empty. Instead, Ki drove his ax blade into the wrist bone of the other, who howled with pain. Ki snatched the lantern from his hand, lashed out with his gun barrel, laying him out, then hurled the lighted lantern into the streambed, now flowing with kerosene. A flicker of flame raced down the incline past that small, heavily guarded arsenal.

"Put out that fire!" a guard began yelling. "Quick! It's the powder house!"

Ignoring the commotion caused by the spreading fire, Ki headed directly for the cabin where Jessie and Adriane were being held captive. His sprint brought him across that bullet-swept interval unscathed. A gunman serving as a sentry in front of the cabin came at him, leveling his single-shot Springfield rifle. Ki swerved. The guard triggered and missed. Ki caught the long rifle barrel and jerked the man toward him. The gunman dove for Ki's legs, almost upsetting him, but Ki reversed the rifle and clubbed the man, even as the hurtling form shouldered him aside. Ki, catching his balance, grabbed the guard, spun him and dashed him headfirst to earth, then clubbed him again. Hastily, then, Ki searched the comatose guard's body for weapons, finding no pistol, but taking a skinning knife from a sheath. Its tapered, thin blade was razor-sharp, and though he desperately wished he had his vest with its multitude of *shuriken* and daggers, he supposed the knife was better than nothing. It'd have to be!

Before rushing inside, he glimpsed the chaos in the valley behind. Flames were licking at the base of the arsenal, and quite a few gunmen were rushing that way, some with blankets, others with coats to beat out the flames before they could reach the powder. Other guards were fighting the Chinese slaves, swearing and roaring commands that were washed out in the tumult of battle. Their weapons flamed, and slaves reborn into men—those in the leaping front ranks—went down. But more leaped over them, screaming tirades of invective, swinging clubs, and firing stolen weapons. The guards, guns empty, could not stem that tide of hate. Ki's heart turned to lead, though, when he saw Greg Nehalem, making a valiant effort to reach the cabin and join him, abruptly go down in that struggling heap of humanity. But there was nothing Ki could do now. The distance was too great. And besides there were Jessie and Adriane.

When he crashed into the main room of the cabin, where shortly before he had been brought with Jessie, a warning screamed out:

"Look out, Ki!" It was Adriane's fear-shrill voice.

A gun flamed almost in Ki's face, and pain streaked along his ribs. He ducked aside, catching a glimpse of Tobias Pembroke with a smoking revolver in his left hand, his teeth bared like an animal at bay. A step in front and to one side of Pembroke, Quaid Ruther was cursing as, one-handed, he trained a double-barreled, sawed-off shotgun at Ki. And as Ki threw himself to the

174

floor, he saw that both men were using women as shields. Pembroke had Jessie in an arm lock and was forcing her to back with him toward the inner door, which led, no doubt, to a rear room and an exit. Ruther had hold of Adriane, whose face was bruised and tearstained, and whose once neat gingham dress was in tatters, exposing her taut-nippled breasts.

All this Ki saw in the instant it took for his body to hit the floor. And then the rim of the table at his right mushroomed into cascading splinters from the thunderous eruption of Ruther's twelve-gauge.

With a horrified cry, Adriane slumped, fainting, to her knees. The movement loosened her from Ruther's grasp, and she toppled against him, deflecting his aim, so that his second shot at Ki crashed ten feet from him. Ki dove under the table, twisting around with the guard's skinning knife. There was very little room to maneuver under the table, and getting the right whip of the hand to strike with the skinning knife would be difficult. But he had no intention of trying to beat Pembroke's next shot or Ruther's second shotgun load by leaping head-on at them. Let them come to him.

Ruther, leaving Adriane sprawled on the floor, lost no time coming to Ki. The shotgun barrel and then his face poked down from above, his expression a gnarled melange of rage, bafflement, and smugness. The way Ruther was angled at that instant allowed Ki to snap the skinning knife with a wrist flick that sent it slashing from Ruther's hairline to his chin. His nose, protruding sections of his upper and lower lip, chin hair, and a chunk of the chin itself—all sheared off, as though leveled by a woodworker's plane. Ki ended his slicing stroke with the knife buried in Ruther's breastbone, and when Ruther collapsed to the floor, he fell on it, driving it in deeper.

By the struggling noises in the next room, it was evident that Pembroke was beating a hasty retreat out the back with Jessie in tow. Ki crawled out and stood up, hearing those noises and Ruther's wheezes. Adriane sat up to laugh then, not insanely or hysterically, but with vast relief.

"Get Pembroke! Never mind me, Ki. Kill Pembroke and get Jessie!"

Ki needed no urging. The rear door of the cabin was wide open, and he rushed through, oblivious to his own danger. Outside, the din was increasing. Just as he reached the rear stoop, he saw Jessie glance back at him, anger and fright in her eyes; Pembroke was dragging her along, one arm encircling her slender waist. Even if Ki had had a gun, he would've been helpless to fire, for fear of hitting Jessie. He was vunerably exposed to Ruther's gun. And Ruther was bringing it to bear, preparing to fire.

Suddenly the flaming arsenal erupted. In the violent concussion, Ki was sent reeling. He saw Jessie and Pembroke thrown to the ground, and guards nearer the small cabin tossed about like matchsticks in a tornado; then a vast gray cloud of wood and powder smoke billowed across the scene, blotting all from view. Neither he nor anyone else could venture closer, for ammunition stored in the building was going off and slugs were buzzing everywhere.

Dazed, Jessie struggled to her hands and feet, glancing around. Vaguely she saw Pembroke scuttling away, trying to make a break for the side of a cliff. She started after him, running hunched as low as she could, eyes watering from the smoke, legs weak, and her head buzzing from the shock of that blast. But she kept going, doggedly determined, knowing that if Pembroke were allowed to escape, all this bloodshed would have been for naught.

Ki, too, saw Pembroke hastening from the cloud-wreathed ruins of the arsenal. Then he saw Jessie, and though gratified that she'd come through the explosion, he was frustrated that he couldn't get to her, or after Pembroke. The clash between the Chinese and their captors was raging all around, cutting him off. There was something terrifying about the haggard mob of slaves charging madly at the gunmen, filling the valley with a din of crazed yells, eyes feverish, clothes torn and bloody—a crowd of screaming devils from the bowels of hell.

Jessie was oblivious to the battle as she pursued Pembroke. She made out his rotund outline scrambling up the cliff. Climbing after him, she called out, "You're through, Pembroke! Finished!"

Pembroke's response was a pistol shot that went wide.

Jessie dropped flat anyway, hugging the incline.

Lifting her head, she saw Pembroke moving again, so she got to her feet and thrust upward. Pembroke was slowing, she perceived, age and his luxurious style of living having sapped his vitality. Still, she didn't want to risk losing him, so in an attempt to catch up; she straightened and skittered in a loping run diagonally across to a more solid outcrop of stone. Pembroke fired, once more forcing her down.

Then, as Pembroke paused to reload, Jessie began to climb in earnest, clawing for boulders and drawing up between them, only to reach and grasp another, gravel and broken shale sliding out from beneath her feet. Pembroke aimed by the noise of the shale sloughing down from her grappling climb. His bullet clipped the rock next to her left hand, spitting tiny slivers of stone into her face. She could taste the blood oozing from the myriad tiny cuts, but refused to waste time wiping her face. She groped for the next highest rock, then the next, until, gasping, she drew level with Pembroke.

"You!" Pembroke snarled. "If it hadn't been for you—!"

"It would've been someone else. And it wasn't only me."

"True." Pembroke lumbered slowly toward her, his revolver leveled directly at her belly. But that was all right; Jessie had her twin-shot derringer aimed at Pembroke's gut, too. "But I was betrayed! Betrayed by stupidity, by cowardice!"

"*A chi fa male, mai mancano scuse*—the wrong-doer never lacks excuses. Put the gun down,

Pembroke. Your killing days are over."

"No, my sweet! It is *guerre à outrance*—war to the uttermost!"

Pembroke fired with the speed of a striking rattler. But Jessie had been watching for those telltale signs in the eyes, in the mannerisms, and caught his reflex even before his finger completed its move. She sprang aside, Pembroke's bullet grazing her sleeve. Her derringer spoke once, and more to the point.

Pembroke twisted, his second shot blowing a hole in the side of his own boot as he went down.

Walking over to him, Jessie cocked and aimed her derringer for a final shot, if needed. *"Omne vitium in proclivi est,"* she murmured. "All the roads of vice are downhill . . ."

★

Chapter 12

The battle was over, but the slaves were like madmen. They pulled the main building down, log by log, and destroyed the equipment inside. Others ripped down the gate and fence, piled the poles, and lighted them. Flames leapt high, and they danced around them, capering wildly. Some of the cabins took on the look of field hospitals, with Lieutenant Wolcott, who knew something of first aid, directing help for the wounded. His troopers took charge of guarding the remainder of Ruther's and Pembroke's forces who had escaped the bullets of vengence.

Gregory Nehalem, his arm and head bandaged, was propped up on the floor of one of the cabins. Adriane Bryce was spooning him hot broth; there were tears in her eyes, but she was bravely trying to keep a grip on her nerves. Nearby sat Fong Lu, also cut down in battle. He had wounds in both legs, but he, like Nehalem, would live. Now he was already making plans with two of his countrymen for restoration of the rights of the Chinese prisoners and the return of their property seized by Ruther and Pembroke.

Quaid Ruther lay on a table, his chest and what remained of his face wrapped in bandages. When Wolcott entered to check on the wounded, he examined Ruther and then exchanged glances with Ki. "He won't pull through."

"Good," Ruther croaked in a weak voice.

Now Ki begged him to clear Greg Nehalem of the murder charge that still hung over his head. "Do one decent thing before you die, won't you?"

Ruther cursed feebly. "It happened just like I said. Nehalem shot the ol' Chinaman in the back." A shudder ran through his body then, followed by a gurgling death rattle, and stillness.

Nehalem was ashen-faced. Adriane clutched his hand. Wolcott looked grim. It was clear the thoughts that were spinning through all their minds. Nehalem would have little chance to have his record cleared. Ruther, the chief witness, had refused to change his testimony by a death statement. Hacho Chown was dead and so were the others who had been with Ruther at Fort Younger.

Just when they had given up hope, Jessie and four Chinese entered carrying Tobias Pembroke's huge form. The fat man who had dreamed of fortune and power was a pitiful sight, blackened and burned from the arsenal blast, bleeding from a bullet wound through his lung and from the self-inflicted injury to his foot. Lieutenant Wolcott was about to speak, but Jessie lifted a hand for silence and had the Chinese lay Pembroke on the table alongside the body of Quaid Ruther.

When Pembroke saw the corpse at his side, he

gave a shriek and tried to rise, but Ki held him flat.

"Ruther confessed," Ki told Pembroke. "He claimed it was your idea for him to murder Fong Wah."

"It was not," Pembroke whimpered, gritting his teeth in pain. "Ruther followed Fong Wah to Fort Younger. He killed him, then framed the murder on Lieutenant Nehalem. I . . . I had nothing to do with that."

"But you had plenty to do with other things," Jessie charged.

"It was all a mistake," Pembroke blubbered. "*Ignorantia facti excusat*—ignorance of the fact excuses; when honest errors are made, criminal intent is lacking—"

"Oh, shut up!" Jessie snapped disgustedly.

Later, however, she recalled some more foreign phrases, which she had learned at private boarding schools, and one in particular that she'd learned from an Italian lover met while traveling abroad. As she and Ki were viewing the wreckage of the fortresslike sulphur mine, she thought of men like Pembroke who sought to gain power through their own evil designs, only to go down in defeat at the hands of those they had tried to enslave.

"*Chi troppo abbraccia, poco stringe. Con svantaggio grande si fa la guerra con chi non ha che perdere,*" she remarked to Ki. "He who tries to seize too much lays hold of little. One fights at a great disadvantage with those who have nothing to lose."

183

Watch for

**LONE STAR AND THE REDEMPTION
MASSACRE**

137th novel in the exciting LONE STAR series
from Jove

Coming in January!